Praise for A Little Annihilation

"Scenes from the war live on as trauma in the memory of the next generation. *A Little Annihilation* by Anna Janko is an extraordinarily personal and powerful account of how the worst wartime atrocities affect ordinary people and are seldom recorded in the official histories."
OLGA TOKARCZUK

"*A Little Annihilation* explores war and the relentless grind of history on a human scale—and as such, it is a haunting word of warning for the present and the future."
European Literature Network

"This is a book about children in war and how we inherit trauma—factual and unflinching, but touching and tender ... As with Svetlana Alexievich's reportage, in this book war is shown not only as a tragic episode in history, but as a living memory, which even after many years puts us on our guard as a danger which could recur."
Lithub

"An exceptional book. Exceptional not just because we believe the author when she speaks of her 'genetic trauma,' but due to the powerful language which conveys her sadness, anger, and goading irony, while verging on cynicism. Emotional truth emanates from this book."
Gazeta Wyborcza

"This book argues strongly against the view that instances of war-related trauma can be ranked in a hierarchy."
Wprost

"Janko has masterfully combined her mother's memories, accounts from other members of the family who could tell their own versions of the story, and references to academic texts and essays with her own testimony about inheriting such memories and facing the burden and restrictions they impose."
Onet.pl

"This is powerful testimony. It is our duty not only to read it, but also to pass it on in turn ... Perhaps so that never again will another child be a witness to such horrors."
Babelio

"War-time trauma can be carried over to the next generations and Anna Janko creates a powerful story of her inherited fear. This is a daring book about dealing with the painful family memories of World War II and the Holocaust, and about processing the hereditary trauma which has become part of Janko's DNA."
ANNA BLASIAK

"This shocking yet tender story rendered me speechless for several hours. Anna Janko drags her family's tragic past out from the recesses of memory, but she also provides us with a lifeline."
WIOLETTA GREG

"Janko's book digs deep into the past and into memory to examine the poisonous influence of family trauma throughout the years. It's a harrowing journey, and a painful look at the fate of children in war. What makes the book so compelling despite that is the sheer amount of historical, creative and emotional work that we witness Janko doing in order to process what happened."
MARTA DZIUROSZ

a little **annihilation**

anna janko

a little **annihilation**

Translated from the Polish
by Philip Boehm

WORLD EDITIONS
New York, London, Amsterdam

Published in the USA in 2020 by World Editions LLC, New York
Published in the UK in 2020 by World Editions Ltd., London

World Editions
New York/London/Amsterdam

Printed by Sheridan, Chelsea, MI, USA

The quote on p. 136 is from *The Iliad* by Homer, translation by Samuel Butler, accessed from classics.mit.edu. The quote on p. 175 is from "Hitler's First Photograph" in *View with a Grain of Sand* by Wisława Szymborska, translation by Stanisław Baranczak and Clare Cavenagh, copyright 1995 by Harcourt, pg. 145.

The translator would like to thank the Polish Book Institute for a residency in support of this project.

Library of Congress Cataloging in Publication Data is available

ISBN 978-1-64286-066-5

First published as *Mała Zagłada* in Poland in 2015 by Wydawnictwo Literackie. This translation reflects minor changes to the Polish edition, in agreement with the author.

This publication has been supported by the © POLAND Translation Program

Twitter: @WorldEdBooks
Facebook: @WorldEditionsInternationalPublishing
Instagram: @WorldEdBooks
www.worldeditions.org

Book Club Discussion Guides are available on our website.

The beginning

Just think, Mama, it could have been worse. All they did was kill and set things on fire. No torture, no cruel torment or physical abuse. They didn't even rape the women. They just came and killed people, one after the next. And since they did a sloppy job—hitting some and missing others—they sometimes had to make corrections. Good thing they used guns, too, since death from a bullet is supposed to be the best kind. Plenty of people can only dream of dying that way ...

Mama, just think, your father didn't suffer for more than a moment, and your mother not at all—one minute she was there and the next she wasn't. They never even saw your new home burn down. Never even found out that the whole village had been burned down and that almost everybody they knew had perished. They were lucky.

*

I'm either imagining or else I'm remembering. I can say this because fear is a type of memory—something inherited, passed on before birth and sucked in with a mother's milk. Fear that is supposed to protect the infant from danger.

I remember that day because your nightmares shot straight through my umbilical cord into my bloodstream, while I was still inside you. After all, you dreamed about it constantly: you had no other way to shake off that horrific sensory overload—the images of blood, the loud flutter of fire and human screams—which you drank in with your eyes and ears when you were nine years old and experienced an apocalypse. And you experienced it fully conscious and aware, because nine years is old enough for tragedy. Except you didn't know any language to fit the crime, so you couldn't tell anyone—until I was in your womb and able to hear the story without the words. Later on, once I was already in the world, we learned the words together ... And so the story from your childhood became the core of my own. That's why I remember that day as though I had experienced it myself.

Following a cold and windy May, the first day of June dawned after a deep, short night. As the darkness slowly faded, the sky parted from the earth. Then a few brighter patches appeared—the final flush of blossoms on the trees in the close-packed orchard. A dog started barking, and was soon joined by a second, although they should have still been sleeping. The sun was already climbing the hills so it could peer down into the narrow valley. And in the valley was a village: eighty-eight houses, most with thatched roofs. Two or three made of stone. And that one single house with a shake roof and wooden walls on a stone foundation—our home. Number 57, on the north side of the street, because the road ran from west to east and the houses were constructed along its axis.

Sochy.

That was Tuesday, June 1, 1943, around five in the morning, in the village of Sochy, three kilometers from Zwierzyniec, nineteen from Biłgoraj, twenty-seven from Zamość, eighty from Lublin, two hundred thirty from Warsaw, six hundred ninety-eight from Berlin, as the crow flies. Eight light-minutes away from the sun ...

The sun was barely standing on its rays when high on

the slopes north and south of the village, and far off on the road from the east and from the west, figures emerged as though from a bad dream.

*

You were still dreaming. I know you remember that last dream of your normal life ... You're with your mother in some town, on a big square full of people. A huge crowd, a sea of people, which sweeps up your mother and she vanishes from your sight. You look around and call out— in vain. Then there are fewer and fewer people, just a few lone individuals walking around, and you're standing under a solitary tree, calling out "Mama! Mama!" at the top of your lungs. But she doesn't hear you, no one hears you, your shouting has no sound. In dreams things happen as though inside a glass jar, removed from the world.
   You are terrified.

*

Do you know that I remember a similar dream from my childhood? As though it were a twin of your own. I first had it in Stolnikowizna, where your mother's family lived. You and Papa used to take me there, but never to Sochy. Still, it's the same part of the world, some forty-odd kilometers towards Lublin; your father used to cover the distance on his bike. Once—I couldn't have been more than five years old—Papa took me to Stolnikowizna; I don't know why you didn't go with us. We were living in Rybnik at the time, in Silesia, evidently you stayed at home.
   The child was exhausted after the long trip and so they put her down to sleep. There were two beds in the room,

both made up. I can still see it: they were at opposite walls, one with red-checkered bedding, the other with blue. I don't remember which one was mine. I dreamed that I woke up and my father wasn't there, that he'd left me there in some house I didn't know. He went to the bus stop without me, boarded the bus, and rode away. I chased after him, crying out. But he didn't see or hear me. I ran after the bus as it was driving away, shouting at the top of my lungs "Papa! Papa!" but he didn't hear me because my shouting had no sound. In dreams things happen as though inside a glass jar, removed from the world ... I was terrified. When I woke up from my dream I ran outside. And there was Papa, sitting on the bench in front of the window just to the left of the door. He was here! He was sitting with Leonka, your mother's youngest sister, and her two daughters, Jadzia and Tereska, had squatted down next to them. Everybody was bathed in the still, dark-golden light of the setting sun.

Later I had the same dream many times, only the bus was sometimes red, sometimes blue ... The blue buses go to heaven, the red ones to hell. That's what we used to say when we were little, back then the buses were either the "Jelcz" brand or "San"—and they were painted in just two colors: red for local and blue for long-distance.

*

What color bedding did you have in Sochy? You don't remember. How much does a child remember from the war? If she was three—like your sister Kropka—nothing. Everything that happens to a three-year-old sinks into the unconscious. For a five-year-old, like your brother Jaś, there are a dozen or so images that his memory shuffles and scrambles, shuffles and scrambles ... A nine-year-old like yourself is fully mature for tragedy: she carries the heavy tome of the war, where the words *the end* are inscribed on the first page. What color bedding did you have in Sochy? Was it red?

*

You used to take me to Stolnikowizna, but never to Sochy. Except we never stayed more than two or three days, because I would invariably get sick and we would have to escape. When I was a baby you had me christened there, we have a photo commemorating the occasion: Leonka is holding a swaddle sack, surrounded by some dark figures. Everybody looks incredibly serious, as though it were a wake and not a christening.

Right after coming back from the church, somebody noticed the child didn't look good, that she had red spots all around her mouth. Maybe from the holy water? Maybe it wasn't fresh? But an hour later the same red spots showed up on her stomach and back, and the child had to be taken out of her bedding and kept naked because she was bawling so. It turned out that the child, who would later become me, was allergic to the land of her ancestors from her very first moments of life. And the only cure for the terribly itchy rash and the swollen throat was to escape from the countryside around Zamość.

The powdery, cocoa-brown loess, which can be carried off by the wind, had entered my being through my mouth, my nostrils, and through the pores of my skin.

We went there a few times when I was little—but always came right back; I would return covered with spots, squirming because of the itching, and howling with pain. Many years later, when I was in my teens, I once again tried spending my vacation there. But during the night I tossed and turned in the feather bedding, scratching my inflamed calves and stomach with both hands. And during the day I'd stay inside, lying in bed, because my throat was so sore I didn't want to do anything. Everybody else went out to the field to gather the flax, while I tried to recuperate, without success. I only got up to look, to watch them bending over, cutting, tying the small sheaves, and then I'd go back inside, sweaty and sore, and struggle to swallow some beets or cabbage. Usually there'd be two huge pots with vegetables on the stove in the kitchen, waiting for Leonka, her husband, and my cousins to come in from the field. There were flatbreads, too, stacked one on top of the other, but they were too hard for me to get down my throat. I had to abandon everything and escape.

That was 1974. However, before I got sick, before my body remembered it couldn't be there, I managed to take a walk around the village. Back then a few of the houses were still covered with straw and painted sky blue. As I was walking I met an old woman wearing a headscarf, a wandering fortune-teller type who predicted I would have two husbands and a traveling life. We met just past the bend in the road, right by the empty house that had belonged to your mother's parents. The road was a lovely dark-brown shade of mud; a few geese were scampering along the edge down a narrow, over-plucked patch of grass that had soaked up water like a sponge. They were hissing because they were scared, but, being geese, they were scared and aggressive at the same time. They were scared because not far off a young man was revving the engine on his shiny black motorcycle, just to show off. He was wearing a white Crimplene suit, with gold buttons. Back then that was the ultimate Sunday chic.

Before the war a couple of men from "our" villages had

emigrated to the US, including one of your uncles on your father's side—what was his name? Everybody referred to him as "the brother in America." That had to be how the white suit with the gold buttons wound up in that little muddy village—inside a package from the USA.

*

In any case, I managed to visit my great-grandparents' house before my rash broke out. The place had been abandoned but wasn't yet falling apart, and I went rummaging around inside. The wardrobe had weathered gray, and creaked when I opened it. A chest treated me to a multi-layered odor of mildew. The mirror above the kitchen table had hazed over; I looked at my reflection and had the impression I was deathly pale. I imagined that you had looked in that same mirror thirty years earlier, when they brought you there, after Sochy was burned down. I felt I was looking straight into your eyes, that your reflection was still captured inside the mirror. If mirrors had memories that they could activate and set into motion—who knows, perhaps no one would have come up with the idea of making films ...

I paced around on the uneven floorboards; when I squatted down, the cracks between them widened and I noticed a bluish bead and a hairpin. I sat on a chair which must have once been white but was now streaked and spotted. I wanted to feel something, but I didn't know what. Some other time. Some other me.

And I did feel something. Like a holiday feast without the celebrants. As though I had happened upon the traces of a past civilization, which I had left ages before and where no one was waiting for my return, because their time passed ten times faster than mine.

When I stepped outside to head back to Leonka's house, I was attacked by a rooster. A giant red rooster with a comb like a piece of bloody meat. It was waiting for me on the porch and as soon as it saw me it jumped up fluttering and clacking—as if directed by Hitchcock—and sank its beak into my knee. I screamed and retreated back inside before it took off flying. With shaking hands I bolted the door. Leonka had told me earlier that the place was guarded by the neighbor's rooster, and that the bird claimed the abandoned homestead as his dominion, but surely I wasn't going to take a story about some rooster seriously! Meanwhile he regarded me as an intruder who had barged in on his territory.

I sat imprisoned in the empty home for quite a while, afraid to venture out. My knee was bleeding, and fear had me by the throat. After time had slowed down a bit and my emotions had subsided, I dashed outside and ran limping through the yard to beat the rooster who was right then heading for the barn. I slammed the gate behind me. Was I from this place or wasn't I? Nothing here wanted me.

Two weeks later—that's how long I was able to bear the rash and swollen throat—they put me on a wagon and carted me to the bus station in Wysokie, then in Lublin I boarded the train to Wrocław (you remember back then we were living in Wrocław). For months I kept looking at my girlish legs, disfigured with bluish scars from the scratch wounds, and I swore I would never go back.

*

It was only recently, meaning as an adult, that the allergy abated. In 1998 I took a trial trip to the Zamość region. When the train reached the Roztocze hills—"Tuscan" is how the tour books describe that area, the Polish Tuscany, because it's easier to appreciate one beautiful thing when it's compared to a better-known beautiful thing—and the windowpanes were passing through green-yellow fields scattered on the slopes like checkered scarves, I was moved. To be honest I couldn't keep from crying. The tears flowed out from somewhere deep inside, perhaps they weren't even my own. In fact I remember thinking it wasn't me that was crying, but my genes.

Something similar happened a year later, when the Hungarian folk band Téka was playing in the old town in Warsaw. Your father had Hungarian ancestry, though any material trace from the time his ancestors arrived from Hungary was lost long ago. I was never particularly interested in that history, although I was happy now and then when a child would be born in our family who didn't look very Slavic—because in my mind dark eyes and a swarthy complexion were always a promise of beauty. Your father's father, for instance—your grandfather from Sochy—was a handsome man with a black mustache that never turned gray ... Or your cousin Czesia, also a Ferenc. And my own children—dark-complexioned, with black eyes.

It was only by chance that I happened to hear the band Téka that day. I was in the old town market square, standing in a crowd of people who were listening, but I probably heard more than they did. Because something started playing inside me and merged with that music. I felt a longing—even though I couldn't say for what, and for no reason I started sobbing so intensely that I wanted to get away. And I wasn't some old woman recalling bygone days—I was still young, starting a new life in Warsaw, with a new man! But in that moment I was unable to control myself, and out of the corner of my eye I caught puzzled glances from the people around me; they probably thought I was in pain or else had some worries beyond the music ... After all it was just a band playing Hungarian folk tunes ... Meanwhile those sounds were affecting me, circumventing my conscious mind, and reaching into—I don't know—my identity? Hidden, ancient, but spirally inscribed into every cell of my body.

And did you know that *téka* is a Hungarian word for shelf, a particular shelf in the home, a special place for family keepsakes, documents, photographs? I recently came across the translation of that word, just by chance. And see, what a surprise, I have Hungarian rhythms in my blood. From you, from your father.

And those were the mornings on the first day

Your memory has faded and so much has slipped away that today I remember more than you do. I've also asked around and done a little reading. We need to sit down together so we can recover as much as we can. After all, it's our shared story, our shared history. Sometimes it strikes me that now it's more mine than yours ...

*

That morning, when your mother woke you from your nightmare, you were happy to see her and felt overjoyed that she had found you. But your relief lasted only a few seconds. You woke up and for just a moment everything was the way it had been, and then reality turned back into a nightmare from which there was no waking.

"Wake up, Renia, get the children dressed," you hear your mother telling you. "We have to get out, the Germans are in the village—do you hear—they're burning houses, taking people away." You do hear, and you see your mother running around, grabbing this and that, bouncing off the walls of the room like a bug in a jar. And you see her terrified face in the pale early morning light. You jump up, grab the things drying on the string beside the stove, and toss them under the bed. Under the bed? What are you doing, Renia? You have to get dressed!

After that ... you don't remember.

After that your mama probably dressed the children herself—Jaś and Kropka (they were the "children" since you were already a big girl ...). And then she was outside in the yard saying to you, "Come here to me, through the window, you're going to take some sacks and cover the windows to the basement." The basement was lined with stone. You covered the little windows with potato sacks. By then your father had taken everything inside the basement so it would be safe: the feather bedding, the pillows, the blankets and winter boots, his sheepskin coat, and his bicycle.

After that your memory is once again blank.

*

"But you do remember your mother taking the holy picture (the one that protects from fire) off the wall and blessing you with it, don't you?"

"I remember her making the sign of the cross with that picture."

"Then she leaves the picture behind and takes the three of you outside. Through the shop, because that way led out to the yard. There's shooting and screaming. You can smell the smoke."

*

At the Ferenc's across the way (where your cousins and grandfather lived, house number 56, on the south side of the road)—in other words, at your cousin Staszka's— Aunt Anastazja was the first to wake up. Staszka was nine at the time, just like you. She remembers her mother looking at her, and that was enough to roust her from her sleep, as though her mother had actually touched her. Her mother is sitting on the bed with her eyes fixed on Staszka, but she doesn't see her daughter because she's using her eyes to listen and not to see. After a moment Staszka also starts to listen, she hears banging and cracking sounds coming from outside the window. One at a time, then two at once, then one after the other again. They both listen, looking at each other with unseeing eyes, until her mother turns to her father and shakes him by the shoulder. She shakes him once, twice, but he doesn't want to get up. The children are faster, they're right on their feet, without shoes. Staszka's mother tells her husband loudly that something's going on, that they can hear strange noises, but he says, "Don't pay that any mind—it's probably the springs squeaking, what with the way Grandfather rolls around in bed." And he turns back to the wall. After that Staszka's mother runs to the window, then to Uncle Antek in the other room, then back to Staszka's father and shakes him by the shoulder: "Get up, the village is burning, we have to get the children dressed right away, let the cows out to the orchard ..."

*

Stefka's mother (Stefka Skóra, twelve years old, number 83) cried—she forgot you're not supposed to cry in front of children—she cried and repeated, "Hurry and get up, something bad is happening, hurry and get up. The Germans are coming down the hill."

They could hear shots, and buildings were already on fire. Stefka's father ran outside to let out their cow, then went right back inside to get the children. He fell to the ground, shot, and lay there in the yard.

*

Danusia (Ziomka, five years old, number 42), woke up all of a sudden and her first thought was about her bunny rabbits. She rushed outside to open the cages—the frightened animals were huddled in the corners. Then her uncle, who lived in the same house, also ran out, shouting, "O God, save us …," and fell. Their neighbor, who was carrying his little son, also fell. The boy dropped from his father's shoulders, rolled a few feet, then crawled over and hugged his father, begging, "Get up, get up, get up." But his father didn't get up.

*

Staszek (Popowicz, thirteen years old, number 47) woke up when he heard someone shouting, "The village is burning!" He jumps to his feet. And with him Edzio (three years old) and Marynia (five years old). His mother tells him the livestock has to be driven out to the orchard, but Staszek sees Germans coming down the hills one next to the other, rifles ready to fire.

And suddenly it's a very long way to the orchard …

*

Fourteen-year-old Marysia (Szawara, number 55) was awakened by a rifle shot. She sits up to look out the window and manages to see the neighbor woman topple over and not get back up. So she jumps out of bed and runs out together with her sisters to hide in the rye.

*

At number 88, four children saw their mother get shot and drop to the ground. Their father immediately flies into a rage and throws himself at the German who shot her, tears his rifle away, and smashes it on a tree. Straightaway another German kills their father and three of the children, sparing only little Leon.

*

Franek (Szawara, twelve years old, number 11) and his family spent that night in the barn. He was roused from sleep by his father's shouting: "Get up, the village is burning!" They got up and ran to save their house. His father was shot before he could make it. His mother fell, wounded, then a German who was coming through the yard finished her off. Next the German fired at Franek's sister Feli, killing her; she was sixteen years old. Then he shot Franek's other sister Justynka, who was eighteen, several times in the stomach; she was six months pregnant, she survived. After all that, she gave birth to Hania who was "mentally unfortunate"—that's what people later kindly said about her instead of "mentally ill." Hania Hatalska never saw her father, because he was also killed that morning, age twenty.

Franek's uncle, Staszek Szawara, who was also your uncle, lived at the same house, on the west side. He died then as well, and his wife (your father's sister) suffered some kind of hemorrhage and died a short time after, leaving their two daughters, five-year-old Janka and three-year-old Czesia. It's that same Czesia who takes after your Hungarian grandfather: black eyes and hair—a real beauty.

*

"The Nizios lived at number 25—the parents of Bronka, the one who later became a folk poet. Interesting, isn't it? You're a poet and so is she, one 'literary' and one 'folk' ... Do you remember her? Bronisława Szawara she was called, because she married a Szawara. Your families must be related."

"That's the way things are in the countryside, half the people are related and the other half are in-laws ..."

"Exactly. It was Bronka who numbered all the houses that had been burned down. She described them in her poem about Sochy. House by house. Who died and how, who was left. Later, after the village had been rebuilt, the numbers were reversed for the new houses, perhaps as a counter-spell to break the curse ... Back then, in 1943, Bronka was fifteen, which is a lot in terms of life, so she was able to recall quite a bit more than all of you. Even what happened during the days beforehand. And her mother was the seamstress your mother used to go to, remember?"

"Mama would pick up a blouse to be mended or some fabric to make a dress for me and we'd go to the seamstress, mostly just before evening.

"That Katarzyna Nizio was an intelligent woman, she subscribed to newspapers and read books, was curious about everything that was going on in the world, she was full of information. Bronka also had a little sister, Marysia, and you used to play with her on the floor by the legs of the sewing machine."

"We would play with the snippets of fabric that fell. Make different patterns ..."

"Like children today put together puzzles."

"So her name was Marysia?"

"Yes, Mama, I checked, it was definitely Marysia. She survived, too. And there was also Stasio, her middle brother, he didn't. Bronka stayed very connected to Sochy; she just passed away a couple of years ago. She's the one who told me what went on the days right before it all happened, how people sensed something was in the works. As early as Sunday there'd been noises about the Germans deporting people. Bronka's father heard it when he passed through Aleksandrów—which isn't very far away—on his way to his sister Hałasicha, who lived in Rudka. She'd been burned out of her house some time earlier, and he was going there to help her finish her new home. After the fire they'd built a little house, and there was still one room and the basement left to complete, so he used to help her in his spare time. That's why he wasn't home that Sunday when the neighbors came in the evening and sat down on the porch and started whispering about something."

Bronka told it like this: "I'd just walked back from a May crowning in Tereszpol, where we did a lot of singing around the statue of the Virgin, and I saw Wicek sitting on the steps talking with Józef the cobbler's son. But I was worn out after all that celebrating so I laid myself right down to sleep and I don't know what those boys were whispering. And here at night something comes clomping up to the porch. Mama asks who's there and what do you want and that something answers that it's Father: open up. And what are you doing coming back at night? And father answers, they say there's Germans moved in on Zwierzyniec. Jasiek saw it coming back from work, some kind of soldiers swooping in and everything's all running around and such a ruckus there in Zwierzyniec it's frightening. So Father wanted to come back right away. That Jasiek Hałasa, Hałasicha's husband, took him out to Biały Słup. I'm going to go home, Father says to him, but they'll ask for papers and I'm not from here, so better take me out to the path that goes to Biały Słup. And so he took him there. The main road passes through that way. And in the dark he took that road back to Sochy. And the next night was already June first. It was just starting to turn gray outside and we heard some more knocking. Who's there and what do you want? It's Stach Jaroszów knocking at the window and he says there's something moving in the hills, zigzagging from one side to the other. That was the Germans. They'd gone by train to Szozdy and they were stirring around, lining up ... And all of a sudden there was a shot and you could see smoke. The smoke was there right away because they were firing flaming bullets. Go, tell the children to get up, Father says, the village is burning. A couple of places are already on fire, says Stach Jaroszów. Dear Lord Jesus, and our loft had already been robbed by them that were hiding in the forest! That's where we hung up the washing to dry. Something's already burning over by Masztalewicz's and we can see smoke at Mazur's. Go let the cow out, Mama says to me, and to Father she says, you hitch up the horse and ride out to the yard. Father points at Marysia: I have a few coins here, he says to Mama and me, tie them to that holy medal she's wearing, they may take her off to Germany what with her being so small, so the child has something for bread, and write out a card so they'll know what her name is ..."

*

"How much time did you have in Sochy, Mama? Fifteen minutes? Twenty? In some villages it was only five. People had five minutes to get dressed, bundle up some food, grab a rosary and a little pillow for the child and move out right away, because otherwise the Nazis would break in and burn them down together with the house."

"What do you mean Nazis!"

"OK Mama, I won't say 'Nazis,' I realize no one there knew the word, they just said 'Germans,' and everyone understood what was meant—namely fear. Of course in Sochy they didn't give you any time at all, because you didn't need it. Their only plan as far as you were concerned was killing. No one took any documents out of your hands, this time no one was deported anywhere: for death you don't need an ID.

"When I was little I sometimes used to imagine I was you, little Renia, getting out of the house that morning with my mother and little brother and sister. All the people in the village are doing the same thing: they're escaping outside, running out of their homes—eighty-eight houses—and into their yards, while the Germans are filing down the hills, shooting from above, and setting things on fire once they get a little closer, shooting all the while. And here you are spreading that blue apron on the grass! It was decades ago that you told me, but to this day I can't forget that image. Every time I spread out some blanket or sheet—anything—for just a split second as I'm making that same gesture I become you, with that apron dropping to the ground ..."

"That was Papa's work apron for the store, why I took it I don't know. Maybe because there was dew on the grass and my dress might get wet? We get outside and make it to the narrow lane between our yard and the neighbor's and I have this blue apron with me and I just spread it out on the grass next to the path. Blue against green ... And I sit down on this apron. No, I don't sit down, I lie down. Anyway, somehow half-sitting and half-lying I look around. A soldier goes by with a burning bunch of straw and holds it up to the roof of the house next door. Where the blacksmith lived. Evidently the Germans missed the blacksmith's house when they were shooting the flaming bullets. The blacksmith's wife is standing there, she puts her hands up over her head. My father is next to her, by the fence, a few meters away from us. He asks a different soldier who's standing there with a rifle if he can go back inside to get some money. The man nods that he can. The blacksmith's wife says 'Don't go.' Papa shouts across to Mama who's with us: 'Let's go to their place (meaning across the road to his brothers and my grandfather), I'll just get the tin. Whatever they have in mind (meaning the Germans) applies to us as well.' The tin had the day's receipts. Our home had a shop.

"The blacksmith's roof was soon in flames because it was straw. Ours was wooden shakes, so it wasn't burning yet. That holy picture was protecting it.

"And then my mother says, 'Papa just fell so he's probably dead.'

"I look and see Father lying on the path, at most five steps away from the fence. 'Maybe he's just lying down,' I say, because it could be that way. I want it to be that way.

"And already the Germans are coming towards us, two of them, in green army uniforms, with garrison caps. I don't remember their faces, just their uniforms against the sky. As if they didn't have faces. But what I do remember very clearly is the gesture, how one of the soldiers aims his rifle at Mama, who's standing on the other side of the path, right near the rye, with my sister in her arms. And even before my mother's legs start to give way, that soldier points his rifle at the child.

"And then the other one ... then the other one pushes the barrel to the ground. All I remember is that movement, I don't remember the shots, as if there wasn't any sound. Mama goes to the ground, the rifle goes to the ground and fires into the earth. And my brother and I are on that apron two meters away. Everything happened so close, we were all within a few meters, but it felt like we were on a huge empty square … Maybe that second soldier was a father himself and so he didn't want a child to be killed?"

"Maybe. Maybe he felt that whoever kills a child is also killing his own child a little bit …"

"My sister is lying there in the rye. Her eyes are wide open, she's still alive. My brother is sitting next to me."

"He told me he was standing, not sitting."

"Never mind what he said … It was horribly quiet. As if everything had suddenly stopped happening. I can't see my mother but I know she's lying close by. I don't remember how she was lying. I get on my feet and feel an ice-cold shockwave pass through me on the inside, and from then on I'm a completely different person. I take my brother and sister by the hand and we head down the path towards the road. We walk past our father. He's lying on his back and there's a hole on the right side of his jacket, where the bullet went through. I remember thinking: that's where the bullet went through. I saw his Adam's apple moving, as though he were swallowing spit. He had on his new brown herringbone jacket, and the hole was in that new jacket."

"Your brother remembers it differently, that he was lying on his stomach, and that the hole was on the left side, near the heart."

"Jaś was only five, and I was nine, so who do you think remembers better? Kropka doesn't remember anything. And she saw it too. She hid it all somewhere under the surface … It was a different soldier that shot Papa, not the one who had nodded his head, and not the one who set fire to the blacksmith's house. Maybe the same one who shot Mama. Papa kept the money in a tin box, and he must have hidden it in the basement that morning. Maybe he wanted to get it to buy our way out of the deportation camp, thinking they were going to cart us off to Zwierzyniec, the way they had done with the people in Wywłoczka some two months earlier."

"But that wasn't what they had in mind for you."

"We walked past Papa, his throat was quivering, as though he were swallowing spit. I instinctively wanted to swallow, but couldn't. As if I had a stick in my throat. We are orphans—the thought was looming over me—everything was horribly quiet."

"Jaś remembers the same thing, that he didn't hear anything."

"And I walked on. We didn't stop when we passed Papa, I just couldn't. I had to keep moving, step by step, it was the same response as when a person is too paralyzed to move. I was paralyzed but kept on moving with the children and with that one single sentence in my head: we are orphans."

Little Renia

Little Renia. Big gray eyes. Straight hair with bangs. A round mouth. Cheerful. Active. The first child of Władek and Józia Ferenc from the village Sochy. Her earliest memory is of crawling across the threshold of their house, then lying down on top of it, hoisting first one leg across and then the other, and there she is, on the other side. The threshold must have been quite high. And Renia must have been quite little. That was before the war. Since she was born in 1934, the latest that could have been was 1936, before the birth of her brother Jaś or her sister Kropka. And that house didn't belong to them, because they didn't build their own until 1938. Up to that time they lived with one of Władek's sisters, the same one who leased him a room for the store. Władek hadn't received any land from his father, because there wasn't enough to go around for all five brothers—Władek, Staszck, Antek, Michał, as well as the brother who left for America. Two sisters, Maria and Agnieszka, completed the Ferenc clan.

Prior to 1846 there's no mention of any Ferenc in the various lists pertaining to the Sochy villagers, for instance in the archives of the Zamoyski Estate, not even in the recorded disputes over timber ... Perhaps they didn't arrive until after the 1848 Spring of Nations, when masses of people were on the move in that part of Europe. And they didn't necessarily come directly from Hungary, because the name Ferenc shows up in many parish registries from the Podole region as early as the seventeenth century. Supposedly they left the area around Lwów even earlier. And Sochy wasn't the only place they settled, because the name shows up in various places throughout the Lublin province. Here one decided to stay, there one decided to move on—for example to Małkinia, where Andrzej Ferenc's family comes from. I'm sure you know who I mean, he's that actor who reads poetry so beautifully. He told me he comes from a long line of artisans. That explains something, because my grandparents and uncles were all hard-working, resourceful, enterprising people: blacksmiths, carpenters, gifted with their hands. When my grandfather was young he had this idea of keeping a shop, and so he set one up. It did quite well before the war, and even later on it didn't do too badly, given the circumstances. Until the last day. It's Grandfather Władek I have to thank for my strong chin, an anthropological trait associated with a strong will.

*

Władek really loved his Józia. She was cheerful and endearing and so petite he could lift her with one arm. He liked her best when she wore her green headscarf, because it made her look like a little girl. She was very good to him, to the children, even to the cat prowling in the pantry. She didn't let their red-haired dog Misiek be tied up; he roamed wherever he wanted. And where he liked most was next to the stove, watching to see if something might fall near his muzzle. O that Józia! They met in Ruszów, when they were both working on a farm to start earning early on. She had two sisters in Stolnikowizna, and he had five siblings in Sochy; it was clear neither would receive much from their parents, maybe some feather bedding or a tablecloth. Władek was leading the horse back from the field when they first exchanged glances, and he knew right then and there on that country road— he felt something squeeze inside him. They soon got married in the village and waited until they'd made enough money to set up the shop they dreamed of and buy their first wares. Renia was born in Ruszów, they christened her there and entered her name in the church registry, but they'd already decided to return to Sochy and build a house on a little piece of land that Władek's father had given them, across from the Ferenc family home. Near the well with the sweep pole that his father had built for the village.

Eventually they would have a yard, and in the yard they would have a shed, and they would have their shop, their stove. And so it began. At first they lived with Władek's sister, Agnieszka Sirko, since her cottage had plenty of space, and rented a second room for the shop. A neighbor helped them build their house—he's the one who's buried with them, all their names on a single plaque. A solid house, constructed of thick, tarred planks, with a stone basement and a shake roof—not straw. Not too big, not too small, with a separate room for the shop, with space for boxes and crates of goods. And a broad counter that would one day hold big jars of candy.

Their dream was becoming reality. As the house was being built, little Renia ran around the site, clambering on the piles of rocks, the stacks of boards. And in the evening, as they walked back through the village, she would grab her parents' hands and bend her knees so she could dangle between her mother and father and laugh herself silly and shout "Swing! Swing!" Ultimately they had to leave Renia with her grandparents the Mielniks in Stolnikowizna for a while, because there was no one to keep an eye on her, and she might hurt herself or—God forbid—fall into the lime-pit.

Józia was smart and waited until 1938 to have her second child, after they were already in their own house. How she loved that house! She was always adding something, hanging something, setting something out. Here another pillow for the bed, there a doily, a throw for the bench. On the table she placed a big, beautiful cast-iron cross, and she hung holy pictures on the walls. She was so afraid they might get burned by the stove that when Władek was installing it she warned him three times to be careful. And then she hung that holy picture on the wall, to guard the miracle that had befallen them.

Władek had a knack for work, there was nothing he couldn't do, just like his father, old Ferenc, who fashioned various things for his neighbors: benches, crosses, coffins when needed, not to mention the sweep well in the middle of the village. In 1905 he contributed a shrine at the end of the road when an outbreak of typhus came to a happy end. My own great-grandfather. I'm not exaggerating when I say I'm so proud of everything he did that my eyes start welling up when I think of him—with his black whiskers and Hungarian looks, the same man who saved Kropka in his overcoat when the village was razed.

Władek achieved his happiness. And before that evil day, on the first of June 1943, he managed to enjoy life together with his wife, in the home they shared. When he would come back to the house they had for those few years, he would take Józia's hands and whirl her around until the window became a blur and her scarf went flying off. The children would bounce up and down beside them, squealing with joy. He was thrifty, and made sure they had enough for today as well as something saved for tomorrow. Only once it happened that Józia spent money for nothing. Władek had gone to Szczebrzeszyn to buy some goods, and while he was away the photographer showed up in Sochy, where he went from house to house, hawking his services. The whole village had its picture taken then. Józia also wanted a picture with the children, one she could set on the table and look at. And another to take to her parents in Stolnikowizna, so they, too, could look whenever they wanted. That was a miniature portrait of Renia and Jaś, just their two little heads snuggled together. When Władek found out that she'd spent the money he got very angry, what kind of useless idea is that, Renia and Jaś are right here, running around wherever you look, what on earth do we need those pictures for?! He yelled and the whole house went absolutely quiet until later that night. But he didn't hold a grudge, his bad mood vanished with the morning sun. Renia got a kiss and Jaś got a piggyback ride from sooooo high up that he could reach all by himself into the candy jar that was standing on the counter in the shop.

Until the war broke out they didn't want for anything. People paid in cash or with eggs, now and then someone would bring a chicken, and even the occasional goose before Christmas. Boruch, a Jewish man from Zwierzyniec, would come in for eggs: as usual in the country, eggs were in greater supply than money. There were so many that Renia soon couldn't stand the sight of them; she griped and grumbled and hid the yolks in the coal. She was a strong, chubby girl, but not very tall; she didn't really start growing until during the war. They'd been living in their new house for just a year and already people were saying there'd be a war; still, they hoped that it wouldn't reach the village, that their valley would be overlooked. That January the youngest child was born, Renia's little sister Kropka. By then there was less food, and Renia started liking eggs again. She grew fast, and no sooner had she eaten than she was already hungry again. She would watch her mother feed the children and she, too, wanted to eat. Occasionally her mother said, "So go out and fetch some of those egg yolks from the coal heap." And then Renia would go outside, walk around the house, and trudge back, as if from some sad fairy tale. Their last winter was particularly hard; the Germans were requisitioning food from the village, so scarcely anyone went to the shop for anything other than carbide or kerosene, and they had very little to pay with.

*

That's the fairy tale I made up about you, Mama, that's the beginning of the nice story that soon turned into the cruel history of Europe.

"And that little picture portrait, the one your father was so angry about, where is it?"

"It got burned."

"In other words your mother took it with her to the next world."

*

Your mother Józia's maiden name was Mielnik—a name as popular in the eastern regions as Müller is in Germany; it means the same, too. Anyone who had a mill, who ground grain, could be called that. Different Mielniks might live in the same village and not even be related—or might have been at one point in the past. And her father was Józef Mielnik, your other grandfather, the one with flaxen whiskers, as opposed to Józef Ferenc's black ones. After the fire, after Sochy was burned down, that's where

you all went, to your grandfather Mielnik in Stolnikowizna. I have to sort everybody out so I don't get them
mixed up anymore.

If Saint Agata is around ...

A child lives on a very small planet, surrounded by a few close people, a handful of objects. Everything glows with phosphorescent newness, everything amazes just as it is. It is the world of first things, which has no perspective, no context. A child doesn't compare, doesn't draw conclusions from gathered information. A child has a mama, a papa, a sister, a brother, a dog Misiek in the yard, kittens in the shed, one grandfather with a black moustache and another in a different village with a flaxen one. A child has a sun and a moon above the orchard, a tree and a field, a rag doll, a new notebook, and grass for whistling with when you blow through it in a special way.

It's a pretty short list.

So when that child sees her parents killed before her eyes, it's as though her entire world is killed as well, together with the sun, the moon, the tree and the field, the notebook, the doll. Even if her grandfather and brother and sister survived, from then on they'll be completely different, as though they had emerged from the end of time. And none of the things will return to how they were before, even if they maintain their shape. Which they didn't, because in Sochy no stone was left in place. Only the sky, and the earth ...

*

"You don't know which saint protects from fire?"

"I do, because I checked, Mama, it's Saint Agata. 'If

Agata is around, then your home is safe and sound,' 'Bless bread and salt in Agata's name, to keep your household safe from flame.' That's what they used to say in the country, remember? Did you use to say that?"

"No, I don't think so."

"Your mother made the sign of the cross over you with the picture of Saint Agata and sprinkled some salt that had been blessed on your heads, and then you went out of the house."

"What on earth are you talking about, what salt?"

"You said that yourself! Thirty-five years ago you described the scene to Hanna Krall, the journalist who came to interview you: 'My mother sprinkled salt that had been blessed on her three children, but evidently she forgot to sprinkle it on herself and on our father'—that's what you said, at least that's what she wrote down. I found an old number of the weekly *Czas*, which stopped coming out long ago, where her reportage is printed. She won third prize for it in the contest 'Poles Overseas.' That was 1979. You must remember how she came here to Sopot, still so young, with very beautiful eyes ... I don't think she would have made up that bit about the salt. Salt is supposed to guard against death, that's its magic power. So your mother might have done that."

"Nothing of the kind happened."

"Mama, it's possible that you remembered it back then, and that you don't now; it's natural for memory to act up at your age."

"'Poles Overseas?' And for that contest I was talking about Sochy?"

"Yes. You also told Hanna Krall that for nearly thirty years you didn't write anything about your village, and that it wasn't until November of the previous year, in other words 1978, that you sat down and wrote several poems about your mother—all in one day. You even gave her one of them to use in that reportage, because it's quoted:

I

to whom my father is constantly being born
and my mother and the ss-man
to whom villages arise
to be burned down completely at last ...

I

who for thirty-three years am being led to the slaughter
and who did not survive ...

I

... am coming to say nothing
of the slain sob
of the cords wound around my throat ...

"I can't go on, it's such a frightening poem."

"What else did I say there?"

"You took Krall out onto the balcony, pointed at the forest on the nearby hills and said, 'There, that road from Sopot, let's say that's the road to Sochy. That would be where the Germans came from. And here, where these apartments are, would be the village. Right here, in the valley. When I saw this place for the first time I said: My God, can it really look that similar? That's why we moved here, to this settlement.'"

"That's right. And I was telling her the truth. This was the first place I felt at home. We lived in so many places and it was only here that I found some kind of peace."

"And do you remember a certain Sunday, long before the fire (because in Sochy they still divide time into two epochs: before and after the fire), you went with your mother to the church in Zwierzyniec. The Church on the Water, that's what people call it to this day. You remember, don't you? It's a small, white church inside the park, in the middle of some ponds, on a little island, you have to cross a bridge to enter. Zwierzyniec is just three kilometers away from Sochy, it's a straight road through the forest, but you were six at the time and complained that your legs hurt. That must have been the fall of 1939, because your mother was pregnant; Kropka was born that January. 'Mama, stop, my legs hurt, stop, Mama,' you whined, and you kept stopping on the road, tugging the sleeve of her sweater, but she quieted you down and kept hurrying ahead, as if someone were chasing her. A few Germans were walking alongside you—Three? Four? You don't remember. At one point the one closest to you took you by the hand. Amazing. He said something and lifted you up. The dark road you were on, which seemed to lead right to the bottom of the forest, now seemed like a ribbon that the huge shoes of the huge German were pushing towards the back. He was quite a bit taller than your father and in his arms you felt like you were in a giant tree being shaken by the wind. Your mama looked so small from there! Now she walked even faster, practically running, only occasionally lifting her head to look at you. How long did he carry you? You don't remember. Surely not very long, because his colleagues laughed, and shouted something in German.

*

The good German. They existed, too. And maybe it was always the same one? The one who later, on June 1st in Sochy, said to your neighbor Aniela, when he saw her child's terrified eyes, "Run away, you two." "But where to, sir?" she asked, because all around everything was burning, and he pointed to the field and didn't kill them. Maybe it was the same one who pushed his colleague's rifle barrel to the ground and the bullet went into the earth and not into Kropka? The same one who said in Polish not to kill the children? Józef Cielica heard it, he was standing close by. His son Wiesio was two years old, so that was important information. Maybe it was the same one who cried when he had to shoot at the boys and men lined up in the yard at the Skóróws'? Because they say there was one German who cried during the shooting …

When I was little you told me so many times about the German who carried you in his arms!

The good German

A registry of good enemies ought to be compiled. Listing the names of those whose hearts cringed.

For instance, one Friedrich Hassenstein from Göttingen. I read about him in a book about the Wehrmacht. Together with some other boys from his infantry unit he was chasing "partisans" in the east (somewhere around the Pripyat River). The "partisans" included women and children, who were told they were being taken to some performance, but in reality were going to their death. As they were walking, a little girl asked him what was going to happen to them; he told her in such a way that she wouldn't be afraid. He calmed her down, perhaps even stroked her head? No doubt something resembling a smile appeared on her face which was streaked with dust and tears, and for a moment her raw bare feet hurt a little less.

Minutes without fear are priceless. And that Friedrich, maybe at home they called him Fritz or Friedo—not much older than that girl's brother—gave her a few such minutes. But right away he was threatened with court martial: the enemy is entitled to nothing, least of all relief from suffering. Hitler, after all, commanded soldiers to exclude mercy from their hearts and act brutally.

No, Mama, Friedo didn't make it to Sochy, because he was a very young recruit, not called up until September of 1943, in other words "after the fire"... The conversation with that girl must have stayed embedded in his dreams, since he still remembered that moment so many years after the war, and even wrote a letter to the newspaper ...

*

Another good German came to mind. I read a story from the camp in Zamość, where families were being separated as part of the process of selection. You remember that there was a transit camp in Zamość, right? A little girl who wound up there relates—I found her account among many others in a book about that camp—that her whole family stood there in the camp yard, where nothing could be heard except the shouts and sobbing of children coming from every direction. "When I said goodbye to my father and brothers we all cried. Then I saw one of the Germans turn towards us and he, too, had tears in his eyes. I never forgot his face. He told my father to escape, but Papa said that his sons had already gone to the group being sent to Auschwitz and he couldn't leave them alone."

She remembered both faces: her father's and the German's. The machinery of death had brought tears to both.

*

A good German. We have to remember them, because in that memory lies some kind of salvation from the cruelty of the past. It's good if they have first names, and if not, such names should be invented.

Little Edek Markowicz was eight years old when he was driven out with his entire family from Kolonia Staszica, not far from Uchanie. He didn't have any shoes. It was January, very cold, deep snow, and those children were without shoes, because where could anyone get shoes in 1943? Remember, Mama, you had wooden shoes, too, your father had brought them from Zwierzyniec, but wooden shoes were useless in winter. That mother had somehow wrapped her children's feet in rags. And as she did so, she cried. And that's how they went ... They were taken to the camp in Zamość, and then in February by train towards Siedlce, this time without their mother. They got out at Mordy. I checked on the map, it's a few kilometers away from Siedlce, I even drove by recently, since I had a reading there in town. The children who had died along the way were tossed into a pit, and the ones who hadn't died kept going. Edek's footrags got wet and started to come undone, he would trip over them as he walked, in the frozen ground, his half-bare feet getting stuck in the thaw. Then a German escorting the children picked him up and carried him. That's something that needs to be seen and felt—a soldier from the enemy army hugging a freezing, dirty boy to his coarse uniform, or more likely his woolen coat, a boy crusted with scabies and covered with lice. Because how could the soldier not hug the boy once he had started? How else could he carry an eight-year-old in his outstretched arms? There's no other way than hugging. Undoubtedly that Edek's nose was running and he was terrified. But the soldier, let's say his name was Kurt, treated him like a human child. Maybe that Kurt had a little brother? Or had left his own son behind at home? Or perhaps he had a similar recollection from childhood? Or simply had a heart.

*

And who today remembers Dr. Hagen? Wilhelm Hagen was the head of the Office of Public Health in occupied Warsaw until 1943. He was one of those Germans who treated Poles as human beings. Alas, he didn't show the same engagement on behalf of the Jews in the Warsaw Ghetto ... However, he did play a role in rescuing children from the Zamość region, who were deported between December 1942 and January 1943 from the camp there. When Dr. Hagen learned from a secret report of plans to ultimately kill seventy thousand children and old people that no one knew what to do with, following the forced removal of two hundred thousand inhabitants from that region's towns and villages, his hair stood on end. I don't know if you learned about that later, in school after the war, during history—after all if there was one class you should have stayed away from, it was history ...

The plan to remove all the inhabitants from the Zamość region and colonize it with German settlers was both inhumanly cruel and insanely simplistic. They planned to deport two hundred thousand people—mostly to labor camps, but about one third were unfit for work: too old or too young or too weak. Ostensibly there would be pensioner-villages, specifically designated for such remnants, but in actuality the magnitude made it a problem difficult to solve, so that young children were threatened with a "final solution" like the one planned for the Jews. After all, only a few were suited for Germanization: most had anthropological measurements and color traits that were deemed unsuitable. In practice the whole plan was a mess from the outset; only on paper did it hold some ghastly logic.

So when this Hagen learned what that "resettlement" was to look like, he wrote a letter to Hitler himself. He sat at his desk, took a page, and wrote on the top: *Mein Führer!* and on the bottom the date: *December 7, 1942.* Then he wrote that he had heard about this plan, and that he considered the idea to be very harmful for the Reich, from a military-political point of view as well as from the perspective of foreign affairs and population policy. In his letter he expressed the risky view that among all the foreign workers, Poles should be viewed as racially close to Germans and as much less dangerous than the southeastern races. He further argued that one of the Poles' few sympathetic traits was their love of children and that if those children should expire then so would the last spark of hope for an understanding with the Poles, because they are by nature inclined to resistance and violent acts. That's how cleverly he formulated his case. I suspect Hitler didn't answer him ...

Before Hagen was removed from his function and punished by being sent away from the General Government (Himmler even wanted to send him to Auschwitz, as he did with Hagen's Polish colleague, Jan Starczewski); he managed to help save the lives of some of the children being transported in the first ten days of January 1943.

It happened this way: first, still in December, the transports from Zamość passed through Warsaw carrying the young people and adults being sent to Germany to work. Then there were rumors that the children would follow the same route. As Dr. Hagen foresaw, the Varsovians were extremely moved by the children and prepared to risk life and limb on their behalf. They immediately organized clothing, food, and medicine, and mobilized pediatricians to assist. They set up regular shifts at the Warsaw stations in anticipation of those trains (unheated freight cars, for the record), with automobiles standing by to transport the children, along with ambulances on full alert. Everything in plain sight of the Germans, who had already begun to fear disturbances. A number of children were saved when the trains stopped at Warsaw East Station and in Bródno. Some were taken off in return for payment of fifty or one hundred zlotys or some similar sum. They were saved in the hospitals and in the homes of the railroad and streetcar workers. Hagen agreed to let

Starczewski travel to Stoczek as well as Żelechów near Garwolin and evaluate the condition of the children who wound up there: the sickest and most emaciated ones went to the Warsaw hospitals and were rescued.

And that was the end of Dr. Hagen's career abroad. He returned to the *Heimat*, where he worked in a regular clinic ... Jan Starczewski survived the camps. Evidently this Hagen was no angel—he had skeletons in his closet—but thanks to him many children from Zamość were saved. Such good deeds should not go unrecorded: the names of the Germans who performed them should be taught in schools, and films ought to be made of them—perhaps a little different from *Schindler's List* ...

*

Oskar Schindler? You haven't seen it? Impossible. But maybe that's a good thing: it's not a film for you. That Schindler also entered history as a good German. More than a thousand Jews owe him their life, there's no doubt about that. And numbers matter ... But as far as details are concerned it's not so clear. Spielberg, who directed the film, which came out in 1993, shows how Oskar's Nazi heart changes into pure crystal. Gradually and selflessly. In the space of three hours we see a drunken sexaholic become transformed into a mythic hero beyond comparison. In the end we cry along with him. But let's not be naive, that's just a feature film, the reality was somewhat different and it cost everyone quite a bit ... Evidently Schindler left his factory in a car filled with diamonds and other valuables. Which were later stolen from him. And maybe this is just another wartime legend, only from a different angle? The further history moves away from us, the more it becomes mythologized—that's natural. People need myths more than they need the truth, which is usually complicated, ambiguous, and full of internal and external contradictions. Myths offer what the following generations need: a clear storyline in which good triumphs over evil. When the last witnesses graciously depart, all that remains is the myth, which is in accord with deep human need. And the documents rest in the archives or get lost or oxidized. Or else are simply not believed.

It's unfortunate that "Kersten's List" hasn't entered the sphere of powerful myths. Who remembers Felix Kersten? Well thank God there's a book about him, although it's little known. He was Himmler's doctor and masseur, a Finnish German, who, towards the end of the war, thanks to a cunning tactic he employed with his constantly ailing patient, saved around sixty thousand Jews slated to die in the camps. Sixty thousand! Numbers matter, right? But that's another story.

*

Every country has its own myths. That's why the history of Europe is like a puzzle with pieces that don't fit. Because the good parts and the bad parts cannot be reconciled through international discourse. The profit of one man is the damage of another, as Montaigne wrote. In their schooling, German children receive completely different pictures to piece together than Polish or Ukrainian children. One thing is certain: we shouldn't expect change for the better, because there's no such thing as moral progress in history. Do you remember what Agamemnon said to his soldiers before the battle in *The Iliad*? That they had to kill everyone, that the fetus in the womb of the mother had no right to survive. There's no progress in art and none in history, but there certainly is progress in the art of war.

Mothers' wombs, the incubators of existence, where we cross over into existence. And the soldiers, loyal to their leaders, loyal to the cause that demands annihilation even unto the womb, receive the order to do just that ... The men of the ss had an inscription on their belt buckles that said "My honor is loyalty." Nothing more, nothing less. Those belt buckles kept coming undone because of a faulty design (on uniforms fashioned by Hugo Boss). In the middle of an operation— let's say, while a soldier is killing a pregnant woman—the belt would suddenly come undone as a result of the violent movements ... a rather questionable thing to happen with one's honor. And when it did, a soldier would be embarrassed or simply irate. These feral belts must have caused the Waffen-ss designers considerable consternation during the ongoing evolution of the uniform accessories.

*

Let's get back to the numbers. In the Zamość region alone, ss-men, soldiers, gendarmes, and police in service of the Germans pacified 115 villages, some of them several times; they ultimately deported 110,000 Poles (from nearly 300 villages). Of these 110,000, some 30,000 were children, of which 10,000 did not survive. You didn't know those figures, did you? These children died in Majdanek, or in Auschwitz, they suffocated in the freight cars during transport, they froze, they died of pneumonia. It's unknown how many disappeared in Germany, where some arrived who had blue eyes ... And if someone were to separately count the children killed on the spot, in the houses and courtyards? Or the ones who were orphaned, and as a result were half-dead themselves?

Those who were in the wombs of the murdered mothers have not been counted. Your mother was pregnant when she was shot ...

First names

Szarajówka—a little village in the neighboring borough—was pacified somewhat earlier, on the 18th of May. The villagers were taken to the town square where they were interrogated and tortured, all on account of the "bandits," of course. Then they were herded into a stable, which was locked and set on fire. Were tortured, were herded, were set on fire ... The impersonal grammar helps move everything into the realm of abstraction ... But let's put it more precisely: German gendarmes and Ukrainian nationalists stationed in Biłgoraj and Tarnogród did this. Even more precisely: they burned fifty-eight people alive. Among them two-month-old Jaś, one-year-old Julia, two-year-old Marysia, and four-year-old Ania; Bronek and Marysia were five, Janinka two years older—she'd been given a present the day before: a notebook and pencil; Wanda was eight years old and Kostek ten (he didn't like his name, which was after his father's, but his father also perished, as did his mother and his sisters). Another Julia, thirteen years old, another Ania, fourteen, another Marysia, also fourteen. All those first names are real. All those children are real ... every one of them. The children of Szarajówka, killed, "removed" from life, and their names entered into the book with the lists of people murdered in the villages.

But what did those names look like? Did they have braids, freckles, smiles with missing teeth? Black eyes or gray? A collar tied with a bow? Pants with suspenders?

The photographer seldom visited the village. And when he did all the children ran after him as though he were a magician ...

And the names of the murderers? We don't know them. Did they get entered in any list other than that of the good Lord whose mills grind slowly but surely?

*

The names and faces of certain ss-men, for example the ones from Auschwitz, could not be concealed, because there are photographs, albums with a few hundred pictures. Because the camp personnel had great appreciation for the invention of photography and gladly posed for pictures. Karl-Friedrich Höcker, for example, had his private album from Auschwitz, and pasted inside are photographs of his ss-colleagues, smiling and singing, in the company of some girls from the camp administration—all captioned. There's also an album of the victims, showing the prisoners, the freight cars, the barracks, everything. That album came into the hands of a young prisoner named Lili Jacob, a Hungarian Jew who discovered it after the camp was liberated. The Hungarian Jews were sent to Auschwitz relatively late—it wasn't until May, 1944—but even so, most met with their death. Lili was eighteen years old. She didn't want to give the album away and after the war carried it under the mattress of the baby carriage she used for her daughter. She didn't want to let it out of her hands during the Frankfurt trial either (everyone remembers the Nuremberg Trials, but there were also several others, you know). Because the album contained a photo of her younger brothers, taken right after they got off the train following a brutal voyage. And right before they died in the gas chamber. They are standing on the platform, two little boys wearing pretty, identical little coats. They are looking into the camera, in other words right into the eyes of their sister who survived. Gazes fixed in photographs are always in the present. Even if the people have been dead for a long time. They still keep looking and looking, and that is devastating. They look as if to ask: did I die? And it is you they are asking, you who are looking at that picture ... And they don't stop even if you answer a hundred times, because the dead do not believe the living.

That's the only memento I have, Lili kept repeating, as she refused to let anyone touch those pictures; at most she would show them or possibly make a copy. I'm sure you understand, Mama: there wasn't anyone strong enough to tear that album away from her. The photos provided concrete evidence against those officers, but even so they weren't particularly effective—the punishment meted out to most of the ss-men was hardly more than a slap on the wrist. Because what are a few years, or even months (!) in a civilized prison? What's more, they were often let out quietly before their allotted time. One man sentenced to life got out after eight years—can you imagine? A scandal for the history of mankind. There was no reparation, no remorse. One after the other claimed to be "*nicht schuldig*" during the trial in Frankfurt.

Unfortunately the victims are left without compensation and so are condemned to further suffering. When the perpetrator isn't called to account, the cycle does not get closed and the victim is never freed from the pain— such is the mechanism as researched by psychologists. So death may be a more fortunate outcome. And that's precisely where you didn't succeed, Mama. You survived, but the suffering is always there under the surface. In some sense, something in you is always dying but never becomes dead. That little death is sitting inside you, whispering, frightening you all the time. Those soldiers and ss-men who changed the course of your life returned to their homes, to their children, but they didn't talk about the war in front of them, since war isn't a subject for children. They clipped the war right out of their awareness with one clean cut, because that was hygienic. Only with time, when the sons and daughters of the Nazis grew up, did the situation become more complicated.

*

When I was young I asked you if that German who killed your parents had ever written a letter to you after the war. If for instance he didn't want to show up with some food when you were eating bread with mustard in a Polish orphanage. Or take a few of you on vacation. You laughed out loud and said that he would have been too afraid. "Why?" I asked, surprised. "After all, no one's afraid of children."

"It's not children he's afraid of, it's himself," you said.

And that was all the answer I needed, because it was clear: everyone is afraid of a soldier who kills, even the soldier himself.

The murderers from Sochy were not punished, there was no redress, and so you wrote in your poem: "I ... who did not survive." Because there exist various states between survival and death. And you are living in one of them.

Lili didn't give her album away until 1980; it was only then that something in her grew weary, something let go, and the museum at Yad Vashem received the photographs. At the time, Lili said, somewhat helplessly, of the ss-men at Auschwitz: "I don't hate them, because they have to live with what they did."

Good people are often so naive it's hard to take their side ...

I've inherited enough

Szarajówka, like Sochy, was pacified in retaliation for helping partisans. The Germans hunted down partisans and their families. "Partisan" was a species. The partisan's wife, a girl from the village, and her infant were also partisans. Even Jews could be considered partisans—the category was quite capacious. And all the "partisans" who were caught were hanged or shot. With infants it was enough to step on them. Or toss them into the air and hit them in flight. People don't do those things on their own, someone has to help them. Most likely it's the devil himself, perched on their shoulder and egging them on ...

In July of 1942, Himmler banned the word "partisan" and introduced the term "bandit." He decreed that any aid to them would be punished by death, and declared a policy of collective responsibility. A year earlier he had given the order to raze any village that helped the partisans. He wanted to terrify the local inhabitants so much that they would kill the partisans on their own, or else at least turn them in. Every village leader had the responsibility of filing reports on partisan activity—or after the July decree, on "bandit" activity—at the nearest police station. Every German army and police unit in Poland received those instructions. In addition, if "bandits" killed or wounded a German in a village or even on a road leading into a village, the village would pay with its life ...

*

"I was reminded of this Czech film about Lidice. That's the village not far from Prague that was burnt to the ground, just like your Sochy."

"Of course I know that."

But maybe you don't know that during the 1960s people from Lidice—the ones who survived—came to visit Sochy, to see the same kind of remnants from the tragedy ... Lidice was the only Czech village to be treated so harshly; consequently it's received a lot of media attention. It's famous throughout the world on account of Reinhard Heydrich, the ss Acting Reich-Protector of Bohemia and Moravia, because it was in retaliation to his assassination that Lidice was pacified. There's a well-known monument there, it's quite beautiful. It shows a sculpted crowd of children; there's a figure representing each of the murdered boys and girls ... Poland had hundreds of such villages, thousands of children, so they all get lumped together. And that isn't very memorable, because when you hear statistics about one hundred ten villages in the Zamość region or a thousand in Poland, or claims that, after the Jews, Poles suffered more than any other nation—well it's hard to really picture anything. Events that shake us to the core need to have their own name. They need to be individual and distinct.

And you know, Hitler didn't even feel all that sorry for that Heydrich, he said that it was stupid for someone like that to expose himself to danger. Because Heydrich liked the Czechs, and in his haughtiness he thought it was mutual. So he allowed himself to go riding without a guard and in the end two partisans shot him, not too far from Lidice. And that was the end of the idyll; it turned out that the Czechs were also sneaky Slavs, at least some of them. So they had to be put in their place, which was out of existence.

Two or three years ago they made a film about Lidice. It begins with a love story in a barn. And then comes the tragedy. The most moving sequence shows the children, whose parents were already dead, inside a truck headed to the German camp in the Polish town of Chełmno. It was a truck that functioned as a gas chamber—an auto-apocalypse. Suddenly the truck stops and the Germans direct the exhaust fumes inside, where the children are, and then jump out of the vehicle. One German runs into the field and vomits. I thought cynically that maybe he was sick from the fumes, but then he takes out his pistol, holds it to his head, and fires. The next frames show the little rear window of the truck, the faces of the screaming children locked inside, without audio, of course. The spectators don't hear them and God doesn't either.

I'm pretty sure you won't be seeing that one, Mama, nor should you. I watch everything about the war, but evidently I'm an exception among my acquaintances. For the most part, women my age avoid such films and books. They claim they know what they need to and can't take any more. I used to take the same view, but then I changed my mind. I had to, once I decided to formulate these prenatal stories, filling them out with everything I'd heard during my childhood and later, from you, from others—once I decided to thread the words through the graves of my ancestors. And I tell you, I'm no longer so delicate: I've been hardened. I read documents, watch films, and listen almost without pain to the words of the survivors, now old people with childlike voices. And if one particularly cruel detail causes my hair to stand on end, or my stomach to become a block of ice, I immediately control myself, because this is the work I have to do; it's important for you, especially now that you're starting to forget, and for my children, if someday they might ask me about these things. For the moment they aren't asking. Oh well, these days people generally don't ask about a family's distant past, they prefer to go to the movies or else drink a beer while watching something online—which is so much easier. In the end, history will be written by film directors, and their narrative will become the authoritative version for the average young citizen ...

"And you know, Mama, that in Lidice people are always stealing parts from those children—meaning from those sculptures—to sell as scrap metal? They keep having to solder or glue something back on ..."

*

"I felt a rain of sparks firing into my temples out of fear, and then I couldn't move ..."

"I remember that you told me that after the pacification you kept having this one dream, over and over. There was a dark figure, a dark face, with one smoldering point, like a lit cigarette inside a mouth. The figure bends over you and you wake up with a shout—that's how terrified you are. You don't know who that was? Later you painted him in one of your pictures. A half profile in dark blue with a red glow, very coarse brushwork ... Maybe that's how the German who shot your mother got chiseled into your unconscious? His face—a black smudge ... Maybe he had a cigarette in his mouth, he killed so nonchalantly that he could have easily been smoking. Do you remember something like that?"

"No. Just his cap and the rifle barrel."

"You wanted to give me that picture when I moved out, but I wouldn't have it for the life of me! I was always afraid of that picture; I'll never take it, even if you happen to leave it to me in your will. That's your fear, I don't want it, I've inherited enough of it already."

Don't close your eyes

Fear really is impossible to describe. Once I believed that anything could be described, if you thought about it hard enough beforehand. That by using your feelings you can identify emotionally with the terrible thing you are thinking about, and drag it back to the time when it was happening (or you can remember a different, similar story). Then everything should work out well. Since the Word was there in the beginning, it should also be there later on. But unfortunately this doesn't quite work with fear. Because what words can there be for an emptiness that screams? That screams even as it runs blindly ahead. That screams and runs blindly ahead without moving at all. Like flaming ice that scalds and freezes you at the same time. Words just bounce off that kind of thing like paper arrows, which burn in flight before they even reach their target. There are no words.

*

That's why Aunt Kropka doesn't remember anything. That's what her control center decided. On June 1, 1943, she was exactly three years, four months, and ten days old, and if she wanted to, she would remember something. But to this day she doesn't want to. She doesn't remember her parents. She doesn't remember that day, the first of June. She doesn't remember the following weeks. It's only from later on that a few solitary threads gradually emerge from her memory. A particular moment when she's already in Stolnikowizna: she's lying outside and sees a lark flying off into the blue sky. Or a particular place, for instance a stray sunbeam on the wall at grandmother's house. Splotches of color, like on her tapestries. Because, as an adult, Kropka weaves beautiful tapestries. One of them, fairly large, depicts the valley between Koszarka and Borczyna—those are the hills overlooking the village—and you can see the rooftops of Sochy.

Kropka says that her lack of memory is because her grandfather covered her with his coat and everything disappeared ...

*

"After you crossed the road to grandfather Ferenc's house, where your father's brothers also lived (Stanisław, who was also the village leader, with his beautiful wife Anastazja and their four children; and Antoni, a bachelor), when you got there you said to Anastazja, 'Auntie, Mama, and Papa were killed, Mama is in the grain field and Papa is lying on the road.' A very long sentence. Are you sure that's exactly what you said?"

"Exactly."

"Just then, they and Antoni were letting the animals out of the shed and taking things from the house so they wouldn't get burned. When they heard that, they dropped everything and ran out to the field. You let go of the children ..."

"That's not true, I held their hands the whole time."

"Not true, your cousins say that your grandfather grabbed Kropka and ran. How old was he then? Seventy? More? He grabbed the little one and ran to the orchard. There was a kind of pit there, where they used to light a fire and dry flax or hemp for scutching so it could be spun; he lay down with her in that pit and covered them both with his heavy coat from the first war. Kropka didn't make a peep. The Germans went by, one lifted the coattail and kicked the body lying there. He said 'kaputt' and went on. He went on. And Kropka survived a second time."

"That's not true."

"You think the children were with you. That you lay down together with both of them under the wagon on the field path, and next to you were two other families, mothers with other children. Aunt Anastazja with the little girls, Aniela with four, and Janina with two sons. Everyone was praying. Everything was burning. All right then—so you didn't let the children out of your hands. Let's tell it again in your own words."

"I walked towards the road, Kropka to my left and Jaś on my right. I was in the middle. Above Jaś's head the blacksmith's roof was burning, and over Kropka's head I could see Papa lying there. Then I went across the main road and they were with me. My grandparents were still taking something out of the house. Lots of things were lying in front. I told them what had happened. Then my uncles took us to the orchard. There were these huge cherry trees, full of fruit—so early in the year ... And tall grass. And we got in the grass: Uncle Stanisław with those four children ..."

"Stasia, Julka, Tadek, Helcia?"

"... and Aunt Anastazja, who was so pretty. And Antoni, the forty-two-year-old bachelor. My grandfather in the pit, covered with his coat from the first war. He couldn't have been very old, his whiskers were black, he looked Hungarian. He stayed there lying in that pit until the end. I went on with Kropka and Jaś, I didn't let go of their hands. Behind the orchard on the field path there was a wagon, without a horse. I crawled under the wagon. The

Germans took Uncle Stanisław and Uncle Antoni and the blacksmith. They led them back towards the orchard and shot them. Right nearby lying in the rye was the blacksmith's wife with her family and Władka Szawara, she was pretty, she dressed pretty, she worked in Zwierzyniec, maybe she was the sister of that Szawara who later married Bronka? And her sister was there as well—actually both of her sisters. They were lying next to that wagon where I was with the children. At one point the Germans called for them to come out. The sisters shouted and cried because those men were after that Władka, you know ... But those Germans also weren't so sure they'd have time for anything, one pointed to his watch. They had to make it to the woods before the airplanes came. The sisters crowded around Władka, covering her with holy pictures and with their bodies. They had those pictures. Some of the people did that, they took the pictures from their houses, to save them. Later those girls sat huddled up on the road, crying. Then the first airplane came and the splinters went flying over that wagon where I was. By then I didn't see any Germans, they had already left. 'Take the children and crawl over to us, so if they shoot us we'll be together,' one of the girls called out. So I crawled over to them. The women who were lying in the rye were badly wounded. The planes flew so horribly low that the rye was bent down. I pressed my face into the ground, the roaring was so loud it tore the voice out of my lungs ... That's how it was. Just like that."

*

It turns out Kropka remembers something after all. I asked her to look deeper than her missing memory. And she said that she sees herself lying with her grandfather under the coat, in the dark, with only a tiny mist of light coming through the buttonhole. The buttonhole is big, probably because of the frequent buttoning and unbuttoning. Through it she could see some brown sand and a little grass. Her grandfather whispered to her not to move. That was very uncomfortable for her, keeping still like that. When there was a big roar, her grandfather lifted the coattail and they saw the airplane. It flew so low it was as if it were falling. Kropka was terrified.

You were so worried about your brother and sister that in your memory you are still holding their hands and you have them with you the entire time.

*

Your cousin Stasia, the daughter of the village leader, was nine years old, like you. She remembers it like this: "A series of bullets hit Janina in the legs. Aniela's husband ran down the path towards us, because his wife and children were with us. They shot him. Then three Germans stood over us as we were lying by the path. One was wearing a helmet, another a cap, and the third was bareheaded. Their faces and eyes were red, from the fire. They ordered everyone to get up and pointed their guns at Uncle and Father. The German said very distinctly, word for word, 'Bandits food, bandits vodka, no report,' because Papa was the village leader and he hadn't reported the partisans as he was supposed to, and was giving them food on top of that. The German shot Papa in the head. They also shot Antoni in the head. And they shot Janina who was lying there, also in the head. All the children saw it, the bullet went out her eye. But Janina was still alive. Sometimes—especially if they have small children—a person simply clings to life, although it's not clear how ..."

*

Meanwhile at Bronka Nizio's (who married a Szawara), the one who became a poet like you, everything happened around the wagon they rode out of the yard. But they only managed to go about a dozen meters. There they met their aunt on the road by the house (number 24), she had four small children—Marynia, the oldest, who was five, and Jasio, who was four; she was still nursing one, that was Stasio, and then there was Władzio, who was just starting to walk. And that aunt says, "Take the child, because I can't manage with all of them."

"So I grabbed that Władzio"—Bronka says in her folksy speech—"and my mother took the little one. And we rode a ways into the orchard with that wagon because you could hear the bullets flying. The fire's going to catch us, Mama says to Papa: Keep going a little further because everything's catching fire here—and we can see that the thatch roof is already blazing away. And then all at once a German comes up and we're standing by this crooked wild cherry tree. The German yells to get away, not to get away from the village but *nach Hause, nach Hause*—for us to go back inside, 'back home.' And father says: But sir, everything's on fire! And Mama says to him calmly: Tie the horse here, we'll lie here, there's nothing to be done, we'll have to die, the bullets are flying every which way ... To us, to the children, she says: Huddle into a ball. And to Papa: Cover them with a blanket, so they don't get burned. Because that straw was still flying around and it was furious hot. And to our aunt: Keep that child quiet, give him your breast, don't let him cry, because another German is coming, the one who killed Magdeńka's children, Józio and Kasia, now he's heading our way. But the little one is whimpering, like children do ... We're huddled tight together, all of us lying there, our aunt with her little ones, our Stasio with Papa, me with Mama, and Mama covering Marysia with her body. That German points his rifle at us, I managed to see that much, because I was huddled tight against Mama, then I closed my eyes. Right away there was a shot and I heard something bubbling inside Mama, it bubbled and blood came out of her. Then another shot. I felt flushed with heat, dark, something poured over me and I didn't hear anything more.

"When I woke up the little ones were squealing, and Marysia was crying, she took my hand off my face—the hand that I had covered my eyes with was wounded. Marysia just kept saying Mamusia and Tatusia, Mamusia and Tatusia. And Jasio, our aunt's child, was calling out: Wrap up my leg, wrap up my leg. But his mother was no longer alive and neither was that infant at her breast. They had shot that Jasio somewhere in the knee, later he died in the hospital. When I woke up the planes had already gone by and I didn't see any of that, it was after everything ... Just Marysia was crying: Don't close your eyes, don't close your eyes, because no one's answering, everything's broken, everything's dead, don't close your eyes. And that was all, just those kids moaning and groaning. And our Staś as well, shot three times in the chest and in the arm, he was moaning for water, but there wasn't anything to put it in. When I got up I went looking for that water with my sister because she was afraid to stay. And at the Skrzypy house I found some milk that had been brought there and was in a cup, how was that possible? I took it because I wanted to give it to my brother but he spit it up, it wouldn't go down.

"Then suddenly people are shouting that everybody has to run away, the Germans are coming back. They were coming for their wounded, two had been shot, one was lying up in our wheat field, he'd probably wanted to steal something more and didn't make it out in time before the planes came, and he got hit. People started to run away, and me—what was I to do? I took Marysia, the boys from Szozdy who were coming our way took Staś under the arm and carried him. We didn't manage to take that little Władzio, he stayed there with his mother who'd been killed.

"Soon as I got to going uphill, blood started coming out of my hand so everything began to go dark. We headed to Szozdy so we could take the train from there to the hospital in Biłgoraj. Hałasicha, my father's sister from Rudka, took Marysia, and I stayed in the hospital. And so did my brother Staś. But he was there longer because gangrene got into those wounds. That's what the doctor told him, the doctor said things to cheer him up, that it would be all right, that he'd survive, but he didn't. That doctor's name was Pojasek. The things he had to take care of in that hospital! There was nothing there, nothing to eat, and what was he supposed to feed all those people? He sent me out to pick some sorrel for soup, and asked anybody who came to visit: If you have something to eat, bring it, because the whole hospital is overflowing, both in the surgery and in infectious diseases, and I don't have anything to feed them! To my cousin from Lipowiec he said: Look at those children, how sick they are, bring some flour. And I kept watching for my cousin at the gate, to drink a little milk if she brought some, because she promised, and the caretaker at the gate said to me: Child, what are you waiting and waiting for, yesterday they deported that whole village, and nobody knows where the winds will blow them ... Then my hand swelled up so that the doctor couldn't do anything and they took me to Lublin

to puncture the swelling and take out the bone fragments.

"I never saw Staś again, my brother Staś died ..."

A stroke of luck

So neither Bronka's sister Marysia Nizio, who survived, nor her brother Stasio, who did not, were taken to be Germanized, and her father had been so afraid she might forget her name. They didn't take you either, and they might have; after all, you were pretty; and they didn't take Kropka despite her having blue eyes and hair so blonde it was nearly white—a genuine Aryan. For the children of Sochy there was no clear destiny or destination.

The ones who perished did so either by chance or at the whim of some individual German soldier or policeman. The men from the Schutzpolizei—or Schupo—were particularly lax, they had no regimen whatsoever. Someone from the Wehrmacht said "Don't kill the children" because there were moments when the Wehrmacht soldiers still tried to stick to some moral code, but the police battalions took in a hodgepodge of random characters with a mere three months of mediocre training at best. Not only did they have little idea of National Socialism but they had no concept of any ideology. They were told what they had to do and that was that. They weren't real Nazis, just regular Germans who were unsuited for the real army because they were either too old, were deemed to have defects, or else they volunteered to escape serving on the front. Out there in the East they lived from day to day, without higher aspirations, and were glad to be at Zamość and not at Stalingrad. Apart from murdering people they led normal lives: they visited cinemas and pubs, wrote letters home, played chess. Now and then they even got bored. Probably more than one wanted to see what it was like to shoot a child. But shooting a child is different than shooting an adult, you have to overcome something ... And these men had no special "heart-hardening" training, such as is commonly attributed to those who joined the ss. There was even one soldier in Sochy who cried in the yard at the Skóras' when told to shoot the men who had been herded there. But the youngest person slated to die in that group was sixteen, Janek Pieczykolan, and he escaped. That crying soldier was undoubtedly from the Wehrmacht, and not the Schupo. The assignment caught him by surprise.

All in all a total of forty-five children were killed at Sochy ... And how many survived?

To this day it's not clear how many villagers died. One hundred seven? Two hundred? More? I've even found mention of three hundred. Who was there left to count? People from the neighboring villages tried to determine the number, but that wasn't easy. It was known that a number of people left Sochy at daybreak for their places of work. This one to the brewery in Zwierzyniec, that one to Szozdy where work was to be had on the narrow-gauge railroad. But they were later found dead on the road—the first ones to die, as it turned out. Some of the villagers had left earlier to visit relatives. Meanwhile others came to Sochy to work in the sawmill, or to go to the ponds stocked with fish, or simply to seek shelter after fleeing their villages to escape the Ukrainians. I know you remember that, everybody always remembers fear, and adults and children alike were afraid of the Ukrainians.

People who aren't from there don't share this obsession with counting all the people who were killed, with matching the names to the numbers. The plaques and lists of the murdered are full of mistakes and inaccuracies and there's nothing to be done about it. For instance, your mother's name is wrong and your uncle is listed as Bronisław instead of Stanisław.

What's left is the expression "more or less" rather than individual prayers for individual souls.

*

Those children from Sochy—both the ones killed and the ones who weren't—were lucky. Because they didn't wind up in the transit camps at Zwierzyniec and Zamość, where there was horrible hunger, where lice and scabies devoured the children alive. They weren't shipped to the West, didn't die of thirst on the way. They weren't dumped in the middle of an open field, or shipped off to some German institutional home, with new last names, where they were beaten for every word said in Polish. Nor were they taken to Mordy near Siedlce, as was Edek Markowicz from Kolonia Staszica, or to Pomerania to be bought off a train for a hundred or a hundred fifty zlotys in the best-case scenario. They didn't die at Auschwitz from an injection of phenol, and they didn't eat rancid rutabagas at Majdanek. Except for Stefka.

You don't remember Stefka, do you? She was four years older than you, and that's a lot when you're a child. She lived in house number 8, on the south side of the road—a whole kilometer away from your family. She had two younger sisters and a two-year-old brother Józio. It was with him that she ended up in the camps. The first was in Zamość, after they were deported from Aleksandrów, where her grandmother lived—she had taken her grandchildren in after Sochy had been burned down. Aleksandrów was the focus of constant German persecution, they were always hauling people away from there, shipping them off to forced labor, so people were always escaping to the forest. One day the Germans rounded up the children who were tending cows grazing in the woods.

"I don't remember what day it was," Stefka recalls, "but I remember that Germans suddenly popped out from behind every tree, with their dogs ..." It was very wet, the Germans poured water out of their boots and cursed horribly, they beat and kicked the young cowherds, chasing them through the meadows towards the village. They ordered everyone to sit down above a pit that had been dug out and wait, and they stayed like that until evening; Stefka was convinced she was sitting over her own grave. Then there was the camp in Zamość, and it wasn't until there that she caught up with her grandmother and little brother. They immediately took away her grandmother, so Stefka was left all alone with her brother. They slept in the barracks on the bare ground. Then came the transport to Lublin, after which she was driven outside into the heat and forced to run down Krochmalna Street and further, with her little brother in her arms crying from hunger and thirst. Stefka, out of breath and terrified, quieted the boy down, whispering some promise or another just to keep him from crying out, because if he did the Germans would kill them both. He called for his mother, and she, too, was calling for her mother in her thoughts, after all, she was only fourteen ... She didn't think she'd make it with that child. But she did ... all the way to Majdanek. She passed through all the stations: undressing, shaved head, showers. There, each new day was like the one before. Wake-up for assembly before dawn, German women with whips and dogs standing at the barrack entrance, shouts and beatings. Stefka never made it on time and before she could dress her brother and herself, before both could clamber down from the bunk, she would invariably catch a few lashes on her back. Everyone ran more quickly than she, and she couldn't keep up because of the child. The female guards waited for her at the door as though she were dessert; they enjoyed beating her.

Depraved people like that take great enjoyment playing with a child's sense of terror. Because a child lives closer to the edge of the abyss, and a child's fear is always final and definitive. It's well-known that violence and cruelty can be a powerful turn-on, and what greater ecstasy can there be than toying with the death of another, watching it take shape and ripen. How at first it is shy, not quite believing in itself, how it then grows and grows until it ultimately outgrows the individual victim, and that is what pleases the executioner the most. Watching a death that you have caused to develop is the ultimate trip abroad, an extreme existential adventure. And it always ends well, because the act of killing guarantees that you can beat death at its own game. The victor takes every thing and is left with a feeling of immortality.

At least that's supposed to be the psychological mechanism. But can we know for sure? Where passion reigns, our intellect is weak. There are no words to describe the cruelty of the perpetrator, and there are none to describe the torment of the victim. Not even in the great books of humanity. And because in the beginning there are things that precede the Word, words cannot be the key to unlock such secrets.

And so those German guards had their fun with Stefka every morning as she ran out between them, carrying Józio in her arms, shielding him and ducking to avoid the lashes. The two children almost died of hunger, the water with rutabagas or rotten potatoes was unfit to eat; now and then some merciful soul would smuggle a bit of bread under her clothing for the little one and Stefka would feed him so that nobody could see. Stefka remembers the woman who worked in the laundry, she was the one who gave her that bread. Until Stefka got sick and very early one morning, while it was still dark, they smuggled her together with her little brother out of Majdanek to St. John the Divine Hospital in Lublin. Stefka had a fever, they lay in the back of some truck under a pile of sheets for laundering and waited; someone came and threw a mesh bag with those rolls into the truck. Two children's skeletons, one bigger, one smaller ...

*

"Did they manage to save them?"

"Yes. A stroke of luck in the midst of some great misfortune can be the luckiest moment in a person's life."

Later, after many trials and tribulations, Stefka returned to Sochy. It turned out that while all that was happening, their mother was standing outside the barbed wire, begging the guards to let her in just for a moment, to let her get a glimpse of her children—but by that time they were no longer there. When Stefka grew up and gave birth to her son, she named him Józio, like her little brother, because she had become so attached to him— more like a mother than a sister: that pattern stayed in her head. And you know what? That son of hers lives in Warsaw. He's a journalist and heads a publishing house that specializes in historical books and journals for history teachers. Now and then he runs a commemorative notice in a nationwide paper in remembrance of the tragedy in Sochy, but he's the only one. Interestingly enough, the publishing house that he's in charge of belongs to a German. The paradoxes of history ...

Emptiness

Contemporary psychologists speak of an inner void, an emptiness that sucks away from the inside, without our even realizing it. In all likelihood it begins at birth—along with the amniotic fluid, we imbibe a drop of nothingness that is dense, icy, black. A child's first breath triggers a cry, which is not a shout of joy but a sob of loss, a pleading to go back—it is both longing and fear. Then step by step everything falls into place, though not for everyone. For some people no scar tissue ever covers this void, and they suffer from existential nausea, and wind up harming themselves in one way or another as they try to escape that feeling of nothingness, that fear they don't understand.

And what saved you? In your case, that inner void was suddenly exposed with a single jolt, a single shot—or really two. The protective curtain was torn apart when your father and mother died in front of your eyes. Death came so close it practically changed you into stone. Depression is our psyche's acknowledgement of that emptiness inside our ego. Or in your case: recurring depression. Sobbing, as though a good cry would be enough. Lying in bed, as though a good sleep would be enough. You preferred to sleep, in the belief you would eventually wake up to a happy reality. And ultimately you succeeded. Finally there came a time when you knew before you even opened your eyes that this would be the day, that good day. You got up and began to paint a picture. Or write first one poem, and then another. Sometimes more than a dozen. The poems swept everything out of your soul that was undesirable. It was like a "spiritual cleansing" that converted the chaos into something constructive. The words in the sentences created a sense, a purpose—and that's all that life is about, isn't it, finding purpose? Lots of little ones or a single big one—it makes no difference. Any purpose closes that nightmarish draft that howls inside when the void within ourselves cracks open. Purpose closes it and transforms it into a cozy living space, for a while. Because, unfortunately, the emotional emptiness returns and once again starts dictating terms ...

*

Mama, there's no way you would remember everything exactly, because trauma breaks memory down. Even though you might want to, you won't be able to connect things linearly. Contemporary psychology holds that traumatic events don't produce memories, but rather maintain an active presence. That means everything happens here and now, without regard to the usual passage of time. In other words you go on living your normal life, with things seeming to pass properly from future to past, but something in the background has gotten jammed and keeps repeating. Like a scratch on a vinyl record that causes the needle to constantly jump back to a specific place in the recording. That's where the panic attacks come from, which have nothing to do with the present moment. Or the sudden feeling of abandonment when you're sitting in a house full of people. We, the rest of the family, are sitting in the same room, watching the television, and suddenly you seem as though you're standing in a bare field under a bottomless sky. We look at you and your eyes are like empty screens. And that occurs because what happened to you once long ago was never worked through as it should have been. One could say that your eyes refused to accept what they took in, your unconscious never absorbed it. Some part of your life got stuck in time, like something caught in your throat that can never be swallowed, no matter how many years might pass.

That's why we have to talk about it now. So that it finally gets shut away in the past. So you won't cry out in the night like Staszek Korona—another survivor from your village, who died not long ago. In his old age he no longer remembered any facts, just a child's fear that woke him up at night and caused him to run out of his house. That's why we have to talk through it all, turn it inside out. So that you can at last have peace. So that, God forbid, you don't carry it with you into the next world. And so that I, too, may be less afraid in my dreams. Mama, you don't even know what kind of childhood I had because of that ... It was in some sense damaged. You gave birth to me twelve years after the war and I grew up in the shadow of that horror. That war's shadow never disappears, even at high noon on the equator. And in the night it takes the shape of nightmares. More than once I woke up in a cold sweat because I dreamed a German was chasing me.

*

Your parents called you "Renia." That's nice—Teresa–Terenia–Renia. You're Renia and I'm Ania. A warm-sounding assonance. But I was never as pretty as you were when I was young. My friends said you looked like a French actress. You even looked a bit like the one who played the female lead in Robert Enrico's film *The Old*

Gun—a woman living in famous Oradour-sur-Glane. Oradour is a charming village, almost a town, with stone houses and cobblestone streets that were destroyed in the war. Even one of the ss-commanders felt that his subordinate who oversaw the razing of the village and the killing of the inhabitants had overstepped his orders, and launched an investigation: after all, one didn't to that kind of thing to France. On top of everything it was a geographic mistake, because that wasn't the Oradour they intended to punish—it was a different one, Oradour-sur-Vayres. Can you imagine? They murdered 642 people, turned their home into a heap of ashes, all because they couldn't read the map right. After a couple years of precise warfare a degree of disorder starts to show, perhaps even some hidden madness that lurks inside a person and gets activated when reality crosses a certain threshold of monstrosity.

Enrico's film appeared in Poland in the 1970s, and back then you were at the peak of your beauty. Just like Romy Schneider, who in the film was first raped and then burned with a flame thrower by the Nazis.

"Don't say 'Nazis,' we don't say that."

Okay, the Germans. The Germans burned her. She had big eyes and a perfectly formed forehead. High eyebrows, like yours. A small, slender nose. You also have a slender nose; I was always envious. And when it was let down, her hair fell all the way to her shoulders. Absolutely adorable. After the rape she stands against a wall with a torn blouse, her hair disheveled, and that Nazi, that German, fires at her with a flame thrower. I don't remember much of that film, just the rape scene, and how she screams when we see the flames, and turns first into a burning torch and then into a kneeling piece of coal ... I adored that actress. Very unhappy in life, her son died in his teens in a horrible accident, he was climbing a fence and was punctured by a spike. See how long you've been living, Mama. And we, your children, we've also been living a long time. The ending is better than the beginning, wouldn't you say?

Don't look at them, don't look ...

"That Jewish boy near your house in Sochy ... do you remember him? He must have been hiding in the forest, in
some dugout. Or else he escaped from the camp in Zwierzyniec. It was a year before the pacification. He was coming from the hill called Koszarka. Since your house was
on the north side of the road, and the boy was running
alongside you, he must have been coming from that direction. Do you remember?"

"Yes, I remember it well, the boy was running downhill
through the potato field, he must have been twelve or
thirteen years old. He kept bending over as he was running. What was he doing, bending over like that? I
thought he was playing some kind of game. It was only
when he came closer that I realized he was tearing off the
little fruits from the tops of the plants and cramming
them into his mouth. He would run, bend over, and lift
his hand to his mouth. And repeat the same thing."

"You know those little fruits are poisonous, you're not
supposed to eat them."

"And all of a sudden there were these two big dogs, and
two Germans behind the dogs. Write that in small letters,
that's how it was written after the war—german, with no
capitals . ."

"But that doesn't work, Mama, I write it in lower case
and the computer program automatically capitalizes it.
So where were you standing, when that boy went running
by?"

"Where was I standing? On the road. Between our house

and the blacksmith's. It was as if those dogs simply appeared out of the blue. Because of the hills surrounding the village, the horizon seemed very close, right over your head, like on a tiny planet. Anything approaching the village literally dropped out of the sky, all of a sudden. The boy ran across the road and disappeared behind Grandfather's house ..."

"Grandfather Ferenc?"

"Of course. Grandfather Ferenc was from Sochy and Grandfather Mielnik from Stolnikowizna. The boy ran into Grandfather Ferenc's yard. With those dogs yipping and yapping right behind him. He disappeared behind the gate, and those two Germans followed right after. There was commotion and shouting and barking."

"Did you hear any shots?"

"I don't remember anything else, I was eight years old. They didn't tell me anything, children weren't supposed to know anything. It was early morning, the sun was up, I went outside and that's when I saw him."

*

There was another time when you saw something unusual near your home. In the middle of the day there was silvery-black snow falling from the blue sky. You ran outside on the path and caught the falling flakes in the palm of your hand. They were drifting with the wind, floating and falling, floating and falling, and on some of them you could see strange signs. They were spread out on your palm and you looked at them closely the way you look at a snowflake. But these flakes didn't melt, they just crumbled into ash, into dust. Later your mother explained that the Germans had burned down the synagogue in Zwierzyniec, and that the flakes falling from the sky were little bits from the Jewish holy books. Zwierzyniec is close by, even a child can get there easily, and for the wind it's just one step away, one puff. So it was no trouble for the wind to carry that cloud of scriptures and to squander and scatter them all over the forest and over Sochy. As though, in the fire, that which was weightless and spiritual was lifted from the scrolls of the Torah and the pages of the Talmud and flew away ...

At some point, you don't remember whether it was right after or right before that incident, you and your mother were in Zwierzyniec and you saw those Jews whose scriptures had been burned. They were sitting in the square, very sad, with their bundles, and with their children who were crying. You looked at them, and later the image of those falling flakes from the burned books settled on top of what you saw in the square. And since then, your memory has the picture of the people sitting in the square, sprinkled with ashes falling from the sky, as though they were disappearing in a blizzard, the figures becoming grayer and grayer.

"Don't look at them, don't look," your mother repeated, when you walked by them. "Because they are very sad and full of sorrow."

*

That's what you told me years ago and that's how I remembered it.

*

I'm always glad you weren't a Jewish girl who by some miracle survived, although the fact that you survived was nonetheless astonishing enough. Because Jewish girls were fifteen times less likely to survive: someone made the calculation. For instance Dobcia Kagan, who scratched a letter to her mother on the wall of the synagogue in Kovel, had to perish. As did the girl in Warsaw who a Jewish policeman took to the *Umschlagplatz* when her mother went to the store—she wound up in Treblinka. And she spoke to him so politely: "I know you're a good man. Please don't take me away. My mama just went out for a minute. She's coming right back and I won't be here, please don't take me away."

On the other hand, the little girl in Marian Marzyński's film *Never Forget to Lie* was probably that fifteen-times-less-likely case who came out alive. She appealed to the ss-man who caught her in the entryway: "I'm just a little girl, what do you want from me?" And even though he had a pistol, he started saying to her: "Hold your mouth, don't talk, shut up!" But she didn't stop, evidently that was her personality, maybe in everyday life she was insufferable, quarrelsome, and so she went on saying, "Please, please, don't do it to me, don't kill me." And that German said, "Shut up, don't say anything!" And she said, "If you kill me and I will be dead you will never forget my face, you will always remember that you killed a little girl, an innocent little girl." And so the two of them stood there, the ss-man and the little girl, as though for them the simple machinery of killing and dying had become jammed. They stood facing each other and shouting over each other, terrified by what they had encountered. Finally he said, "Just run, don't talk, run," and he didn't shoot. He was unable to kill her for precisely the same reason that he actually could kill her: namely, out of fear.

Job's second happiness

At one point I knew all that. In socialist Poland the schools made no secret of Hitler's crimes. Children were supposed to gain some awareness about what the Soviet soldiers had freed us from and who our longstanding enemy really was. I read a lot and my awareness expanded to a degree that verged on the pathological.

We all have enemies, that's clear. Even if you're as good as Gandhi himself, it's no use. "So, do you already have your enemy?"—maybe that ought to be the first question put to a child? An ideological jolt like that can really boost awareness. During the Third Reich, schoolchildren were taught anti-Semitism as part of their overall "race education." So it was hardly strange that some little Germanic brat encountering a column of horribly exhausted and starving people (Jews as well as non-Jews) on a "death march" from one camp to another would pelt them with stones or spit on them. After all, their mothers did the same ... They were programmed, the jolt was having its effect, their emotions were closely tied to the enemy the state had provided, and which they used to shore up their own identity on the basis of creative negation.

God, too, has his enemy, which he himself may have created, and with whom he sometimes fights and sometimes negotiates. Perhaps that's the reason he constructed our world, which he uses as a defensive shield. Everyone asks: *unde malum*—where does evil come from? But the answer is simple: it comes from the fact that God has an enemy. Nowhere is that more blatantly seen than when a child is killed. Truckloads and trainloads of children. There can be no explanation. Everyone realizes that this cannot be a human act, no person could do such a thing on his own—something like that would require a far superior being.

*

At one point I knew all that, first from your stories ... You gave birth to me in in 1957 (and 57 was the number of the house in Sochy ...). Our apartment in Rybnik was your first real home after the one that had burned down. Once again you had a family—a brand new one. It was like the story of Job: you were given back what you had lost, only in a different form, a different configuration—you were now a mother and not a child. An odd new fortune, a strange kind of happiness. One that was hard to get used to right away. It seemed unfamiliar, impermanent.

Every time I read the Book of Job I had the impression that Job was only pretending to be glad about his new life, because nothing had been returned to him in a literal sense ... A new home, new children ... How long would it take to grow together? Could they replace the others who had died? Can the chasm of despair be bridged? It was as though the earth had been pulled out from under the feet of someone who was then dragged through hell, placed on the moon, and told: Go on and keep playing, nothing has changed. But everything had changed! Including the fact that the earthly Job had died and the lunar Job was born. The happiness of the lunar Job was taken from the moon. In reality it was a mask of mourning after himself.

*

When God gave you a new home you were twenty-two years old, but in reality you were still nine. As a fraction it would look like this: 22/9. Twenty-two over nine when you got married, at breakneck speed, after knowing Papa for only three months. Then 23/9 when I was born, on August 27 (the number of our apartment in Rybnik!). When you were 33/9 you had a hemorrhage and they operated on you in a Warsaw hospital (your father had died at the age of thirty-three). Before the operation you wove your hair into two braids, because in the case that something went wrong you wanted to go into the next world looking like a little girl. Always the same denominator. The passing years increased; the denominator stayed at nine. What was above the fraction bar changed with the calendar, new life events, the emotions of the moment. What was below always stayed the same.

When I appeared in your life I presented a kind of solution: after all, I was derived from you. You could take me under the fraction bar and talk to me like one little girl to another. I was also a continuation of your life, thanks to some miracle—your life on the moon.

You survived. All survivors have to bear witness. Abandoned between worlds, in the gap between the old life and the new, they build bridges of words, a lunar highway ... And there they reside, even if they have a different, more concrete address and telephone number, work and family ties; they are always in between, with no supporting foundation. You bore witness to me. And when you were thirty-three years old, nearly a quarter century after the pacification, you came through that operation, untied your braids, and started to write poems about those events.

*

And I? Because of all that, it was as though I had two mothers. The first was a mature woman who I missed when she went to the store, who scared me when she was angry, who I was proud of because no one in the whole playground had a prettier mother. And I had a second mother: a little girl who lost her parents during the war, always terrified and alone, who was once starving and had to work for an evil aunt who beat her and made her lug heavy buckets of water up the stairs. It's ironic that one of the best things that happened to that girl after the war was going to an orphanage. That second mother—my little-girl-mother—would sometimes lie down on the sofa and start crying for some unknown reason.

Imagine, a child is looking. A child is looking at her mother who is constantly crying. Her mother doesn't see or hear anything because she's too busy crying. Her face is dark and wet and her eyes are swollen. She doesn't speak as one child to another but rather as though a child to an adult: "Tell me, tell me, what am I supposed to do? What should I do?" Or else she apologizes: "I'm sick, I'm so sick, but it will pass ..." Or she turns over to face the wall— leaving her child utterly alone in the world.

Something was always hurting you. You got tired so easily, you felt claustrophobic in every store and bought any old thing as long as you could do it quickly, and I despaired because it wasn't the dress I wanted, or the shoes, because the ones I wanted were on the next shelf ... But you had already paid, we were already on our way out, you couldn't bear it a minute longer because there was no ventilation. I couldn't stand those clothes, those purchases and those childhood disappointments. I was fifteen when I learned to use the sewing machine, and that was the end of my aesthetic torment ...

Later, when you were diagnosed with heart disease, it

was finally clear that there was a concrete cause for those bad moods, and namely inside your heart—though for the doctors the sickness remained of "unknown etiology" ... But at home we knew the etiology: that June 1st in Sochy. That's where your heart stopped, and when it started up again it was no longer healthy. My little mama—that's how I sometimes thought of you. At times I was mother to my mother. I often felt you needed special care. Do you remember how I proclaimed that when I grew up I would find that evil aunt who made you carry the buckets of water and would set her skirt on fire? I hated the Germans more than you; I felt ready for battle. When I was playing I was always a knight with a long ruler as a sword, or a partisan with a stick for a rifle, or an Indian with a bow fashioned from a clothes hanger. I was all geared for action. I promised that someday I would write a book with the title *Our Mother the Orphan* so that all children would know. Those were the obvious emotions. But underneath there was something less obvious, which ran in the opposite direction and created friction, something that pushed back and acted as a brake. I didn't understand it, I didn't know about psychological conflict, about self-contradiction. I was a child subordinate to my mother; I had to obey her and at the same time I had to mother her and was bigger than she was. I always felt that this particular love was an uphill struggle. "You don't sing lullabies the other way around," I wrote in a poem when I was in high school, practicing my own creativity, when I began to use my internal eye to look at myself through the lens of self-analysis ...

Because how is a child supposed to comfort the child within her mother? How can that scene be staged, how are the arms to be positioned, what lines are to be spoken? Imagine a child looking at her mother who is constantly crying ... I would kneel by the bed next to your wet face, which suddenly seemed so much larger, and I would clumsily stroke your hair and say, "There, there, don't cry, don't cry anymore"—sad that you weren't a doll, because that would have been a lot easier. My mama was alive but somehow unfamiliar, her tears thick as mercury and impossible to understand. And heavy. A mother's tears are too heavy for the child. The child should never see them, if someone cares about their feeling safe and secure. Because that is against the order of things; it's an unnatural feeling, sad, shameful—one that causes existential nausea and cold fear. Lullabies aren't sung in reverse.

*

Now and then I feel you in my body. After all, genes are like a deposit passed from one generation to the next. My body may be new, but the seams, the stitching, the lining, and the outside pockets come from those others. At times I am you, my own mother, when I quickly pass by the mirror and catch your figure and your gaze out of the corner of my eye. I freeze for a split second, because your existence within me runs through me like a shudder. Nothing strange then, that the nine-year-old Renia, who is always alive inside you, is our common orphan.

You didn't want to go back there

You didn't want to go back there, so we never visited the graves of our ancestors, like normal people do. You were incapable of getting in the train and traveling to Sochy for All Saints' Day. Of going there and tending the graves, pulling up the weeds, cleaning the cross ... I can't imagine you would have been able to bend over and clean the gravestone with a rag, or freshen the plaque listing the names, then stand and look up at the little, pale November sun shining from the heavens as though through a stocking. And then bend back down to go back to work. I can't imagine that. All I can see is the little girl you were back then, when your parents were killed, one after the other, and you watched it happen. And then you took your little brother and your little sister by the hand and said, "We are orphans." As if with those words you finished the fairy tale that had been your life until then. And that was the start of a new story—about someone else. Orphanhood is a specific social status, and in the countryside it is one that's felt very acutely. An orphan's lot. Sadness, hunger, hard work, and massive, incomprehensible loneliness. That was what lay in store for you. You were in shock, so you didn't even turn to look at your mother lying in the rye. You led the younger children down the path where your father lay. You had to walk past him. He was lying on his back, in his new herringbone jacket. The whole month of May had been cold and windy, and he'd put it on at dawn so he would be warm enough, just in case. The jacket had a hole on one side, where the bullet had passed through. You looked quickly. His eyes were closed. His Adam's apple was moving as though he were swallowing saliva. But you had to go. There was no force strong enough to stop you. Here, there was no world, no life. You had to cross the road to your grandfather, uncles, cousins: you had to let them know your parents were dead.

*

You were afraid to go back to Sochy, you were afraid that if you stood on the axis of that other world, if you stood on the road between the homes—that world would once again begin to spin, roofs would burn, people would scream, machine guns would spit bullets, and airplanes would drop bombs.

Later it was all forgotten because you had to go through a normal youth and adulthood. School, marriage, your own children, work, maintaining a moderate existence within the poor confines of socialist Poland. There was no time to speculate if it was possible to go or not, if you could stand being in Sochy. Later on came martial law—a dangerous time in Poland. Then the wall of envy between the Soviet Germans and the American Germans was pulled down, and the Soviet Union broke up. Back then you were constantly depressed, you were afraid there'd be another war, and going to Sochy was out of the question ...

Then came the 1990s, which turned out to be a decade riddled with war that provided the news services with a bloody diet. Yugoslavia—a vacation destination for Italians, Germans, and even Poles—suddenly became the site of a bloodbath far removed from the modern, humanitarian idea of Europe. Bludgeoning people to death, right here in Europe? Slitting open the bellies of pregnant women? Throwing children in fires? Swimming in blood in this day and age and in the middle of Europe? Amid all the democracy, air conditioning, nanotechnology, genetics, Grammy awards, deodorants, scientific grants, lasers, clones, space shuttles? All of a sudden the Balkan states reverted to some underlying tribalism; they trampled on the rights of the others to secure their own. Shedding the thin veneer of civilization, they emerged from the depths of the historical subconscious like some shaggy bear whose matted fur reeked of old blood. That's when the depression came back and you hardly got out of bed. Humanity terrified you.

Then the century came to a close—and the epoch of mass killing had a grand finale—practically to the day— on the other side of the world in our new mecca, New York, with the spectacle of the World Trade Center, where death was vertical, symbolic, postmodern. Then we all fell into depression—because we're really Euro-American, are we not? But the close of the century didn't bring an end to the wars, because the new century is spawning new conflicts that keep growing and growing ...

So tell me, when was there a good time to go back to Sochy?

*

I'm reading about the Hutus and Tutsis in 1994. And I'm reading about the Ukrainian massacres in Volhynia in 1943. The paradigm of slaughtering one's neighbors must be deeply embedded in humanity. I'm reading about the Germans who murdered Jews in the death camps. It's amazing how many new books have been published about genocide. As though war moved away in time and then spiraled back in our direction ...

Accounts of women, of children. My eyes widen. I feel panic coming on. I can't sit still, maybe I'll make some coffee. I go to the kitchen, lift the lid off a pot and eat something—I don't know what. I eat a lot, quickly, as if I were hungry, but I'm not. Am I gorging myself on my survival instinct? Maybe better stick with coffee, after all? But in my case coffee after 5 p.m. means insomnia until 4 a.m. ... *How can you be expected to sleep when you learn about such things?* I ask myself. I would like to sleep. Without dreams, just to be safe. I have to get out of the house, something is chasing me outside into the sunlight. Where I can see people, normal people, going here and there, unarmed. Maybe I'll buy a blanket; maybe I'll go into town and buy a light, fluffy blanket, because my legs get cold while I'm reading on the sofa. I really need this blanket. And maybe I'll get a sweater while I'm at it? Reading all that stuff make me feel strangely cold ... Back then the people the Germans rounded up and sent to Treblinka—the Jews, the little girls, the children—they neatly bundled up their sweaters, dresses, stockings, scarves, underwear, bras, all their things, and tied their shoes together with the laces so they wouldn't get mixed up, then ran naked into the passageway the Germans called the road to heaven. And ran to their destination.

*

"But why do you write *Germans* with a capital letter? Write it the way they did after the war, with a small letter."

"I already told you that that won't work, but okay, Mama."

In Not-Poland

There was an irritating French-Polish-German film entitled *The Birch-Tree Meadow* with an aged Anouk Aimée in
the lead. She plays a French-American Jew who returns to
Auschwitz after many years in order to retrace her past.
Fifty years had passed since she'd been sent to the camp,
at the age of fifteen. More precisely: fifty years had gone by
but hadn't really passed. Artistically speaking, the film
isn't the best. Nor is it very kind to Poles, despite a Polish
co-producer: not one is portrayed sympathetically. "I'll
never go back to Poland," states another former female
prisoner from the camp, a French Jew who had been
handed over to the Germans by the legal government of
her French homeland. "I'll never go back to Poland," she
repeats, firmly. As if she'd ever even been in Poland!
Auschwitz is not Poland. It's a transplanted piece of
German skin, grafted onto a Polish body, a Polish town.
Later in the movie, Anouk Aimée says to Zbigniew
Zamachowski, who plays an old Kraków Jew working to
preserve the memory of the Holocaust, that it's strange to
see pseudo-Jewish restaurants being opened, after everything that happened. The conversation takes place around
the year 2000, when Europe and America are full of
restaurants that could be called pseudo-Jewish, pseudo-
Arab, pseudo-Mexican, pseudo-Italian, pseudo-Turkish,
pseudo-Chinese. And Germany also has numerous estab-
lishments of different nationalities, so what's the big
deal? After all, the terrible things that happened did
not happen *here*. Not here in Poland. That's a geographic

illusion. The actual killing, the big annihilation, took place in Germany; the blood seeped into German ground, the smoke from the crematoriums rose into a German sky. At that time it was all Germany. So don't go dropping your victims at our doorstep ... Politics in cinematography annoys me, especially since films now serve as history teachers. Externalizing the crime—that was the German policy and, as we can see, it's been pretty effective to this day. Just like the defense of the military ethos of the Wehrmacht, also carried on to this day, while the youngest recruits from the 1940s are still alive. And they'll defend themselves to the last man.

The pacifist Kurt Tucholsky said it trenchantly: soldiers are murderers. At one point in the 1980s someone imprudently quoted him on German television during a discussion about the Bundeswehr—as the German armed forces are known today—and then it started. The nationwide German conscience was put on alert! After all, it's impossible that nineteen million soldiers were criminals!— referring to the Wehrmacht, the precursor of the Bundeswehr. The matter reached the highest court of the German Republic ...

Of course that's impossible. Just like it seems impossible that so many million people could be killed in such a short time ... But impossible things do happen. If we acknowledge that so many Jews and Slavs were annihilated, we would have to assign a corresponding number of killers, no? In my opinion it would be best if Germany gathered up all the camps they left behind in Poland. So that no one would be mistaken any longer. So that Americans wouldn't speak of "Polish death camps," because when that happens I get so angry I could transport the barracks myself. How difficult could it be, in these times when whole monasteries and palaces are shipped off to other continents? In other words, from a technical point of view, this would be quite possible. The places are dismantled, wrapped in plastic, numbered and loaded into containers. So why not move Auschwitz, Majdanek, Stutthof—how hard would it be? Practically nothing but barracks. And gas chambers. And the crematorium ovens. The mountains of leftover glasses and shoes could be sorted out with no problem, and easily loaded onto freight trains. And the showcases from the exhibits, for instance the camp uniforms and poems written by the prisoners—a mere trifle ...

And then by some miracle also the souls of the millions of people who were murdered, who the Germans brought here from all the countries of Europe—they, too, could be taken west. And people here would breathe more easily ...

*

When I drove out to Majdanek last year, it was early in the morning and I walked around the vast grounds alone. The weather was sunny but cold. I went inside one barrack after the other, where apparently some 500 prisoners were housed in "prosperous" times, and I couldn't shake the feeling that someone was constantly with me. I heard steps behind me and would turn around, disturbed, but of course I didn't see anyone. I bent over to examine the dolls that had been taken from the children during the "welcoming," and froze because I had the impression someone was watching me. I looked around, but there was no one, only photographs on the walls. Photographs of children and teenagers who had died there. And on the opposite wall were photos of the camp staff—the various commandants, doctors, and female "guardians." I took pictures of those photographs. Not all of them, just the ones that would have been there in June and July of 1943. Because if the pacification of Sochy had happened according to the usual model, then after a stay in the transit camp in Zwierzyniec you would most likely have landed here, like the people from other villages in the region. And those were the Germans you would have met. They would have been characters in your life, you would have had to look at them day after day.

Hermann Florstedt, commandant from November 1942 through October 1943—a handsome man, very Nordic; in the photo he's looking slightly upward, with a slight grimace expressing ... irony? He exudes intelligence.

Heinrich Rindfleisch, who was an ss-doctor in Majdanek from March of 1943: *Rindfleisch* means "beef" in German. Glasses, receding chin. Unsure of himself. Perhaps he wasn't cruel? And if he was, it was from fear.

Another doctor, Max Blancke, started working a month before you would have arrived in the camp. Dark hair, fleshy lips, you would have liked him at first; he was strikingly similar to Tomasz when he was young. Forehead, ears, eyes, chin, everything. Which Tomasz? Tomasz N.! —my boyfriend when I was at university, remember, you never forgave me for not marrying him. But if you had met Doctor Max B.—in other words if Majdanek had been part of your biography—then you would not have been able to meet Tomasz, because you surely would not have survived, would not have given birth to me, and I would never have brought him to our home.

Erich Muhsfeldt, who was in charge of the crematorium beginning in November of 1943, felt very much "at home" in the camp. He set up a private room within the crematorium and also a bathroom with a tub. I took a picture of that tub, it's concrete, like the ones in a dissection room. In the photograph, Erich's face looks like that of a corpse who has unexpectedly opened his eyes.

It's very clean in this crematorium, and absolutely silent. The ovens are open, with elongated stretchers sticking out that were used for sliding in the bodies. One girl was shoved in alive on just such a stretcher, as recalled by a man who as a teenager worked in the neighborhood driving a buggy. One day he took a drunken ss-man to the camp grounds. The boy lived nearby, and the ss-man had gotten drunk at the home of a *Volksdeutscher* and had to be taken back to the camp. The girl was Jewish, fresh off a transport that had just arrived. The Germans wanted to rape her. She ran away. The drunken ss-man helped catch her. Then he tied her up and shoved her into the fire. "To this day I can hear her screams," the boy admits (after the war, answering a survey of "experiences impossible to forget"). "That was what terrified me the most."

*

Mama, I'm doing various things for you now so you don't have to. I'm collecting information about the pacifications, photographing each of the gravestones in the cemetery at Sochy—in the end I went there by myself. After all, half the people buried there are relatives, and the others are in-laws ... I talked with Staszka, your cousin, who was also nine years old back then, and with your fellow poet Bronka Szawara, who was fifteen—she recently passed away. And I've been visiting the camps, where I take pictures of children's clothing and of the retorts in the crematorium. You take pictures of flowers and park benches and rooftop turrets of villas in Sopot, while I take my camera and lean over a doll with a crushed face, without hands, on display in a concentration camp. I take pictures of ash piles and camp grounds overgrown with grass.

And that's fair. I do it because of you, because you aren't able to. And for my children, so that they will know. But sometimes I'm not sure it makes sense.

You, too, had a doll with a celluloid face—several, in fact. Your father brought the faces from town and your mother would do the rest. She would stuff out the stomach, and weave yarn into little braids that stuck out so beautifully. Everyone admired those dolls. When I was little you used to sew toys for me yourself. I remember a dachshund you made from a dark gray fabric, with ears trimmed with yellow wool. So you must have had that talent from your mother ...

One three-year-old girl had a doll like that, with braids that stuck out. The girl had blond hair tied with a light blue bow. The girl hugged the doll, her mother hugged the girl, the ss-man tried to tear the girl away from the mother, the mother wouldn't let go. The ss-man shot them both, at very close range. The camp was called Auschwitz.

The doll was certainly stored in the warehouse. Perhaps it was similar to the ones I photographed at Majdanek? Things were easier to save than people.

The warehouses at Auschwitz, for example, contained very many things, including 115,063 articles of children's clothing. Numbers matter ... All those clothes were inventoried before the trains left for Germany, because that country had need of them. Baby carriages went as well. Empty. They were rolled in ranks of five from the crematorium to the train station. The trip took an hour. That was an hour on July 9th, 1944.

Władysław Hasior may have known that when he created his famous installation "Black Landscape I"—a baby carriage filled with dirt into which he stuck several lit candles, and which he dedicated to the children of the Zamość region. I saw that carriage around 1994 when I happened to be at his home in Zakopane for his birthday. The carriage was there—empty, without dirt or candles —shunted somewhere off to the side, in a corner behind the doors. As though it was out of service, used up, consumed by the media, described exhaustively in student papers. A mere shell.

You never went to Auschwitz or Majdanek ...

Majdanek: the crematorium ovens, manufactured by H. Kori GmbH, Berlin. Meanwhile, rival firm Topf applied to receive a patent for a multi-level oven designed to enable continuous cremation, where the bodies would be loaded onto a series of inclines that led to a central furnace at the bottom. I don't know for whom they devised that idea, since by that time most of the Jews had already been incinerated. They even dug up and burned the ones who had been buried earlier. In their factories of dark clouds ... But of course they also had plans for the remaining millions of Slavs ... And thus the engineers toiled on, so focused on their invention that the world ceased to exist for them. That's the normal creative state, which is necessary for progress to occur. And they wound up inventing something truly practical. If the war had gone on, they would have fed the rest of humanity into that oven, like into the stomach of Moloch, because that would have been physically possible.

I'm all alone at Majdanek; it's Tuesday morning. My ears are filled with silence, a massive silence. It pushes against me from all sides, to the point where I can't breathe. Just past the crematorium are some pits: on one day in November 1943 they shot 18,400 people in these pits—Jews. That's eighteen thousand four hundred, in one day, the third of November. The ss-men stood at the edges of the pits with guns. They killed in layers. It turned out that this method was quicker, more than 400 per hour. Mothers with children had to step onto the bodies from the previous shooting, which were still quivering. The mothers carried their children and held them high so that they wouldn't drown in the blood filling the pit.

They held up their children between two deaths.

I think some groundwater must have seeped in, as it did in Łomazy, where the murdered Jews were found floating in red water when the bodies were being exhumed—what else could it be? Human bodies don't have so much blood it would fill a pit the size of a swimming pool.

As I passed the various spaces in the crematorium, completely alone, not a living soul within half a kilometer, I was actually running, not walking, with my heart stuck in my throat. I was hurrying so fast I would have run away and shouted for help if I hadn't come to my senses. That old dread was lurking in those walls. Some kind of extreme emptiness was watching me. I walked around and behind the ovens, to the ash pits. Human ashes were used to enrich the compost for the nearby gardens.

I kept going and going but all I could think about was getting away. Right then, immediately, getting some fresh air. But I had resolved to visit the entire camp, that's why I came, so I reasoned with myself that in this place it was only the dead bodies that perished. But something inside me didn't trust myself and whispered: What about that girl? And what about that two-year-old who got lost? Who wandered about the main square in the camp, hungry, his nose full of snot, crying for his mother, just when someone was bringing in a truck full of corpses to be burned. That someone picked up the child and tossed him on the pile ...

Sometimes people can't bear hearing a child cry.

Burned alive. Better not to think about that. In barns, in homes, in churches—during the occupation of Poland there were dozens, hundreds of such incidents. In the villages around Zamość, older women advised the younger ones to drop to the ground right away, because it's better to get clubbed to death with a rifle butt than to die in the flames ... The perpetrators—in this case Germans—chased people into a place solid enough that it wouldn't collapse under the pressure of the crowd, then set it on fire, making sure that no one escaped. They must have presented a ghastly sight themselves, as they stared at the fire that was reflected in their pupils. They probably didn't hear the horrible cries of the people imprisoned inside, the pounding on the door—otherwise they would have run away.

Later on they said they did hear those cries, but really they hadn't. A long time had to pass before that horrible howling reached their ears. Especially in the evening, when they were alone, with no one beside them to talk to or do something with, and nothing to keep them occupied. Then, out of that emptiness, which hovered above and behind them, a wind started to blow, at first cold, but suddenly turning hot. And that's when the howling reached them. Stopping their ears was of no use: the howls were inscribed in the middle of their brain.

*

I dashed out of that crematorium as soon as my internal guide let me out of her sight, and calmed my nerves with the thought that the original crematorium had actually been destroyed as the eastern front advanced, and that what I was looking at was a reconstruction, as were some of the barracks.

But not the bathhouse.

Not the gas chamber.

They have remained as they were, no doubt about it. I touched the boards of the building, which, even though they had been tarred, were silvered from age. At the exit I stood in the back of the barrack that housed the low, concrete gas chambers and the shower room. And I thought: the same surfaces have traces of the hands of the people who had been here then. I am touching the same thing, in the same place, looking at the same thing. The rest is a matter of time.

I spot a figure approaching on a bicycle. I see a black uniform and a cap. I freeze. I'm standing next to a wall, all alone in a room beside a gas chamber, and a prison guard is coming down the narrow camp lane. Where did he come from? Did I do something wrong? What kind of absurd theater is this?

The figure comes to a stop: he's a strapping, broad-shouldered man, with a pale face—very Nordic. When he addresses me, at first I'm surprised he's speaking Polish, and then I realize that I'd already met him earlier, when I was looking for the barracks of the people deported from Zamość; he had directed me there.

"So," he says, "there's a lot to see, isn't there?"

"There is a lot to see and it's hard to see it," I reply. And then add, "Do you know that from a distance in that uniform you look like an ss-man or a policeman? Couldn't they have made something in a different color so people wouldn't be confused?

He smiles. "My colleagues say it's more like a fireman."

He turns his bike around and points at some new housing settlements beyond the fence.

"And those people there," he says, as he climbs on his bike, "are living on top of a cemetery. They built right over the ash pits."

He rides off, and I feel relief as he does.

*

Hans Perschon managed the gas chambers from July 1942 to September 1943. His ears stuck out so much they looked slightly torn. Devils have ears like his, except theirs are a little higher. I imagine him peering through the small barred window in the ss-men's "little room," evaluating the condition of the women being gassed there together with their children. Because at Majdanek there is such a room, about seven or eight square meters large, with a window at head height, for spying into the gas chamber. The ss-men watched to see if any of the victims were still moving, or if they were already "sleepers." The death squads enjoyed their little jokes ... Today there are two canisters containing gas, as a memorial, similar to the acetylene canisters used by welders. But the ones used here for killing contained carbon monoxide. That's a good death. It flowed in through little pipes along the wall by the floor. There were openings in the pipes. You fell asleep and woke up in the next world with no violence. Some people claim this isn't true, that carbon monoxide in such a concentration causes horrible suffering. Still, if I had to choose among the products in the death shop, I'd prefer that to the other. Because in the other gas chamber they used Zyklon B, prussic acid, in granule form, which left blue stains on the walls and ceiling. Huge blue stains on the gray concrete. First the temperature in the chamber was raised using large blowers pumping air heated to 260 degrees Fahrenheit—and hydrogen cyanide has a boiling point of 78.1 degrees. I didn't know that. I had never known that in my life. I didn't know that the people imprisoned inside were first practically set to boil in that air, and then the pellets were dropped in through an opening in the ceiling.

And their second hell would begin.
Better not say anything.

*

So often we use impersonal verb forms: "they used," "they murdered," "they asphyxiated," "they killed." As if it wasn't done by specific people, but rather by some general evil. Let's rather say, "This Perschon did this, that Hans." The people dying saw his face in the little window. And a certain six-year-old Jewish boy must have thought that's what the Christian Satan looks like. Perschon and Himmler did it, only Himmler participated from afar, remotely. Himmler, who got hysterical when in September 1939 he was splattered with brains during an execution he was attending—because he was not a brave soldier. It took him a while to come to. In the morning, after a night spent ruminating on his weakness, he got up and demanded distance—greater distance between victim and executioner. The procedure had to be perfected so as not to warp the character of those gallant young men who after winning the war would return home and would have to lead normal civilian lives.

*

That image—of splattered brains—is a forceful one, and one which in that war makes very frequent appearance. At Majdanek, guards who could hit the head of a prisoner from a distance so accurately that the brain splattered in all directions received extra days off, to spend more time with their families. During an execution, if such a marksman ventured dangerously close, the brains of the victim might soil his uniform.

I can't remember who wrote about that, I've read so much ... Someone recalls seeing a young boy getting lost in a crowd of Jews being marched in ranks to their death. The boy went up to a soldier and raised his hand, asking to be helped out of the ditch. The soldier led the child away and shot him. Then the soldier's colleagues noticed his sleeve was completely splattered with brains and laughed out loud at him for being so inept he didn't know how to shoot, for having his little Jew-boy right there on his sleeve ...

In Sochy, Staś Popowicz's three-year-old brother was shot in the head like that. Staś, you remember, was supposed to take the cattle out to the orchard across the road and was terribly afraid because he saw the Germans coming down the hill. But then it turned out that he was on the right side, because he survived. From where he was standing he saw the Germans coming down, their sleeves turned up to their elbows ... and then setting fire to his home (number 47). He saw them shoot his mother, his father, his grandfather, his sisters, and his little brother, whose head exploded when the bullet hit, splattering brains over several meters.

"But, Mama, aren't you going to cry here???"

"What's it like when a bullet hits you in the head?"

"It's like a glass breaking, apparently. Someone who got shot in the head and lived a while longer said that. When they asked him, he said that's what it felt like, like a glass breaking."

*

Soldiers also enjoy kicking heads. A child's head will burst at the first strike of a military boot, like a small melon. I read that comparison in the accounts of some

Hutus, probably as recorded by Wojciech Tochman. One of them, who was sentenced to prison, put it that way: "like a melon."

We all try to describe these experiences with words, all the while noting that they defy description. They cannot be described from any perspective: not from the point of view of the victim, or the witness, or the killer. Irrational, but true, one might say.

*

Good thing they didn't mix them together, the executioners and the victims, in that museum at Majdanek. Good thing their pictures are on opposite walls ... Although perhaps it's not good. Because they have to look at each other for all eternity. Particularly the head female ss-guard, Elsa Ehrich, with her cold little smile. As cold as fire is hot. I think there's a full picture of her in a book I have somewhere, together with a group of girl prisoners.

Next to her is Luise Danz, beautiful black eyes, but a grim mouth. The boys at school must have fancied her when she was young. Looks and intelligence—that's pretty much a winning ticket in the lottery of life.

Hermine Braunsteiner seems the oldest of the female guards. She might even look sympathetic, like some dear Auntie Hermine, if it weren't for that thin upper lip. All of these *Aufseherinnen* seem to have something grim about the mouth—I wonder what they would have said about that anthropological trait in Himmler's research institute *Ahnenerbe* ...

There were two more female guards from when you might have been in Majdanek. I shouldn't forget any of them, because it's impossible to know which ones might have been near you if it weren't for a small change in plans, some slackening in the pacification-deportation activities of the Germans. So there's also Hildegard Lächert, with a petite, sullen face, also by no means ugly.

As I take the pictures, my camera makes a sound as though it were touching those photographs. That's what first comes to mind. Evidently the tension I'm feeling anthropomorphizes and brings everything nearby to life. I wouldn't wish that Hildegard on you. If anything, the most good-natured appears to be Elisabeth Knoblich—she looks average through and through.

Eliza, Luiza, Herminia, Hilda, Elżbieta—I'm polonizing the names so that they sound less demonic to my Polish ears. Listen to the names and be glad you didn't meet those women, although they were waiting for you in that place. The girls from the camp called them *katki*—the female form of *kat*, or executioner.

But there was no deportation from Sochy, only extermination. At least all the inhabitants who were shot were spared a hard life behind barbed wire.

Which can't be said about Stefka. Stefka Skóra from Sochy, house number 83, who was fourteen years old and had a two-year-old brother when they both wound up at Majdanek. But you already know that ... It's as though I went there following her path, walking in her footsteps, seeing what she saw. I looked at the circular drains at the bottom of the concrete troughs left over from the washroom, as though I could somehow connect with her gaze that was still there. But maybe the troughs were left over from a laundry and Stefka was never there? I don't know. Today the troughs, in a horrible brown color reminiscent of residue from meat, are simply lying there, under the bare sky ...

The President

Some of the villages in the Zamość region stolen by the Germans—they took over the more affluent ones—had a paramilitary structure. These were known as "black" villages because the newcomers—Germans from Bessarabia with their families—were armed and wore black uniforms. In one such village, on February 22, 1943, the future president of reunited Germany, Horst Köhler, was born. The village was Skierbieszów, which was emptied of its indigenous inhabitants in late autumn of 1942, during the night. They were given twenty minutes to get dressed and pack the most necessary items. Then they were carted off to the camp in Zamość. They were taken through the forests because the German settlers—among them Horst's parents, the Köhlers—were already using the main road. The day had yet to break when the new owners stepped into the open homes. They walked into rooms that belonged to someone else, lit stoves that belonged to someone else, fed livestock that belonged to someone else, and went to sleep in the same beds from which those others had been rousted during the night. Horst was undoubtedly also sleeping in his mother's belly (she was more or less six months pregnant at the time) ... In a big house in the middle of the village, very pretty, with a porch. Inside a room still faintly reeking of mortal terror.

That house belonged to the Węcławik family, who had been driven out with the rest. Ultimately they wound up in the barracks at Auschwitz. Czesław Węcławik's wife Zosia was pregnant, like Horst's mother, and gave birth in the camp. Her baby was "pricked"—meaning the child was given a lethal injection of phenol straight to the heart. She, too, died immediately, after the same kind of injection (in Block 25, surrounded by a high wall, barred windows without glass, bare bunk with no straw). She was twenty-one years old, pretty, with light-colored eyes and full lips, and was named Zosia. It was early in that cold May of 1943 when she went, with her child on her arm, to the death block where she was killed by *Unterscharführer* Hans Nierzwicki.

Someone said that a German doctor threw the child into the burning oven right before her eyes, but her husband Czesław would not confirm this: no one wants it to be so. So let that story be about some other woman's child.

There were several Węcławiks from Skierbieszów in Auschwitz, so I don't know for certain if that Zosia was indeed mistress of the house taken over by the Köhlers, but even if she wasn't, she lived nearby. About a hundred children from Skierbieszów perished in the camp. In order to feel something rather than simply register the number, you have to hear their names and how they called out "Mama" just before being stabbed with a needle. That could all be heard in the neighboring barracks.

Generalplan Ost. Himmler directed its realization from Berlin, while Odilo Globocnik conducted operations from Lublin (where his name is remembered to this day). The planned operation's original blueprint was lost or destroyed—all that remains are sketches and references in other documents. As early as October 7, 1939, Hitler issued a special decree charging Himmler to accelerate Germanization with mass deportations of Poles and Jews. First in the Poznań region, then in Pomerania. Some of those deported wound up in the Zamość district, where they had to endure a second deportation, or were possibly even killed during a pacification. In other words, death merely waited a little while longer for them, and chose a different place.

*

Someone from Skierbieszów recalls that the villagers were given an hour, and not twenty minutes, to pack their things. Then one and a half thousand people were chased onto the square and surrounded by a cordon of ss, while a second cordon surrounded the village. The villagers were made to stand in the cold for several hours while the soldiers checked the list: keeping records gave the Germans a sense of strength, order, purpose, and the general validity of all their doings. Whoever does the counting rules over the counted, isn't that right? I don't know if anyone was shot on the spot there in Skierbieszów. They were carted off to the camp in Zamość; on each wagon sat a German with a rifle. That must have been a very long column of wagons, and a very long trip.

I could easily skip going into so much detail; after all, Skierbieszów is forty kilometers away from our Sochy. But I'm doing it especially for President Köhler's children, so they can fill any gaps in their memory, since I doubt that they've studied the wartime annals of the region, and it's unlikely that German history teachers know too much about it … So what I'm doing for myself and for you, I'm also doing for them. Besides, Skierbieszów is special because of another president who grew up there before the war, a president of Poland: Ignacy Mościcki. The two presidents missed each other in time but not in space … As though the town emitted a particularly kind of energy, like a chakra point that focused and strengthened those boys' political inclinations.

There was a doctor among the deportees, Zygmunt Węcławik, undoubtedly related to the Węcławiks with the nice home in the middle of the village. I found his account in an old book that Uncle Jaś gave me: *Time of Captivity, Time of Death.* That doctor from Skierbieszów describes the arrival in the camp at Zamość like this: "They place us in the square. It's already completely dark. Not a spoonful of hot soup the entire day. A double wall of barbed wire, with barbed coils in between. The same barracks where the Germans finished off several thousand Soviet prisoners. One group goes, another arrives. The quiet wailing of women swelled into a common dirge. The wire gate shut behind us."

That camp was ruled by the infamous ss-man Artur Schütz, a former boxer who reportedly killed children with a single blow.

*

The selection was performed in Zamość. Among the seven hundred people deported from there before Christmas of 1942 to the camp at Auschwitz-Birkenau were forty-eight boys from Skierbieszów between the ages of nine and fourteen; they died from phenol injections. I'm leaving out the girls and the adults from Skierbieszów, including the Węcławiks with the pretty house in the middle of the village, but perhaps President Köhler and his children ought to know about those boys, since it's all part of their family history. Nobody chooses the place of their birth, but nor should it be discarded from memory. Forty-eight is about the size of two school classes, by today's standards. And it's of no importance that Horst's native village (and the former native village of those forty-eight boys) was temporarily called Heidenstein. After all, what

German could possibly pronounce the Polish word Skierbieszów?

*

However, the Köhlers, too, had to escape from Heidenstein a year later, for fear of the partisans, because that
was a horrible year, 1943. Everybody was killing everybody, *Generalplan Ost* was undermined by fear and hunger. Sochy no longer existed; you were already an orphan
... I will only add that in 2004 Horst was sixty-one years
old and that's when he became president of Germany. His
first foreign visit was to the neighbouring country, the
place of his birth, as it were, in what was now again
Poland, although he didn't travel to Skierbieszów then.
What would be the point? After all, he couldn't remember
the time when he was an infant, and he wasn't guilty of
anything himself. But he did remember to say, "I don't
consider myself someone who was expelled. The ones
expelled were the Poles in whose home my parents were
then quartered." Horst Köhler said these words during an
interview in 2007 with the *Frankfurter Allgemeine Zeitung*.
    It is very important that he remembered to say them.
    Debellatio—what a nice sounding word. It means the
complete subjugation of a belligerent nation. In this case
by deportation and extermination. For instance, soldiers
enter a little village, chase people from their homes, murder those who resist, segregate the meek: men over the
age of fourteen (and what mother will say her fourteen-
year-old son is no longer a child?) and young women
(including fourteen-year-olds) are sent to labor in Germany; small children are taken from their mothers—
those with dark hair are killed or placed behind barbed
wire; those with light hair, the pretty ones with Nordic

traits, are deprived of their ethnicity (assuming they survive the transport); older women are left behind, or are also sent to the camp, or else they are shot or burned in a barn, whatever; the family livestock, the provisions, even the seed grain and seed potatoes are loaded onto trucks to provision the army; the village is burned down partially or completely or else preserved for the soldiers' own settlers. Debellatio—in other words: the end.

The deportation of the populace in time of war is against international law, but it seems that no one ever called Germany to account for that faux pas in the military arts. The Germans from Bessarabia, such as Horst Köhler's parents, for example, the "ethnic" Germans—the ones with the black uniforms—also wandered across occupied Europe like people without a home. But they were not without arms. Guarded by ss-men, officially provisioned with goods plundered from Jews and Poles, and equipped with forced laborers who they didn't even feed. Because Poles had to have their own bread to eat and their own horses to work the field.

These "Bessarabians" surely did not consider their lot a happy one. They lived in fear—the same fear they discovered in the homes they moved into—because there was enough fear back then that it both accompanied the ones being driven out to their deaths and also stayed behind with those who came after. They were so afraid, they couldn't sleep. Whole families gathered at the guard station and sat through the night. They had sentries posted on watch. Some of them died as the result of partisan attacks on these black villages. But the harm inflicted was relative, and followed a calculus which stated that if one German was killed, an entire Polish village could go up in smoke, children and all.

The Window

The villagers in Sochy tried hard to spare the children from discovering the horrible thing that happened during the war, but they found out anyway. Using their eyes and ears, and by absorbing it through their skin as well. I remember you told me that you slept under a window, and that the window was a kind of transfer point. And that occasionally at night you would hear voices close by, speaking in short sentences. Then bread and orangeade were passed over your head. You lay there without moving, pretending to be asleep, while gray hands reached in the dark for those gray loaves and gray bottles.

"Papa was handing out those things; after all, he ran a shop and there were goods in the shop. How could he refuse? He would pass them out and Mama would moan: 'Jesus, they're going to kill us, Jesus, they're going to kill us.' He was helping the 'bandits'—the partisans. When it came to food they were pretty ruthless."

"No, Mama, it couldn't have been the partisans, they would have gone right inside, into the store. They wouldn't have reached in through the window. They had weapons and a valid cause."

"In that case it must have been Jews."

"But by then there weren't any Jews left in the villages. The Germans had deported them all."

"There were still a few left, holed up in the forest, in dugouts."

*

That's right, people from the village claim that they helped them as well. But on the quiet; each house had its own dealings and nobody talked about them. Bronka Szawara told me, "Those partisans, they were our own people, the ones from the villages what had been deported, they ran off to the woods, our people and our Jews, later on they'd come by at night to fetch something to eat, some milk or baked bread, once in a while Mama would give a whole loaf ..." That's how you remember it, that the bread and orangeade were also handed out to Jews. "Jesus, they're going to kill us" fits that explanation as well. Because the death that awaited people found feeding "bandits" or Jews was one and the same. You said that up to a certain time (before they deported them all), a man named Boruch used to come to buy eggs from your father. Because in the village people often paid with eggs, for kerosene, for carbide, bread, sugar, salt. Meanwhile your father needed real money to purchase new wares that he would bring back from Zwierzyniec or Szczebrzeszyn. Boruch had a wide basket where he carefully placed the eggs, two in each hand. Today some people say the peasants in the Lublin region were horribly anti-Semitic, that many Jews died at their hands ... Do you know anything about that? Nothing. It's my truth against theirs, you keep saying.

And to back up your truth you point to those trees in the Garden of the Righteous. You know, some people say that those six thousand righteous names don't mean anything, that they're a hoax ... So let's not talk about everybody all at once but about specific people, specific events. This person killed someone, that person saved someone. One acted out of his heart, another out of fear, another for profit. Some people maintain that in a war no one is at fault. Of course that's not true. But nor is it completely false. During war, two plus two does not necessarily equal four, things can cut more than two ways, white isn't white, black isn't black and neither is gray. Because look, those people hiding in the forest—and not necessarily the partisans, but people fleeing the village deportations, and there were plenty of them—those people had to eat, too. At night they went to the windows of the cottages and took what people could give ...

*

"Once they came to our house in broad daylight."

"You never told me about that."

"I don't know, I forgot. My father wasn't there that day; he'd gone to the market in Szczebrzeszyn. They ordered us to lie down on the floor, not lift our heads, keep quiet. I was lying on my bed. I really tried to stay quiet but I was shaking so much the springs were squeaking. They took everything in the shop, including the money. They said that if we breathed a word, they would ... and mimed cutting our throats. After they left we stayed lying there like we were petrified. Until Papa came and saw us. Mama cried terribly and so did Kropka. I ran off to a corner and kept on shaking, holding tightly on to the cradle, so that it started rocking as well."

"Where was Jaś, do you remember?"

"I don't remember, I'm sure he was with us. Afterwards Papa asked us who it was, what they looked like. But Mama just sobbed and shook her head and couldn't say. Papa unloaded the new wares and put them on the shelves. And from then on the money was no longer kept in the drawer but hidden in the base of the cast-iron cross on the table in the kitchen. Mama also stashed some in my dolls, which had little pockets on their backs."

*

So, how can you tell the real partisans from the fake ones? From the prisoners, deserters, and most of all from the common bandits that every war spawns by the thousands (although the word "common" never seemed right to me, given the context). After all, you're not going to ask a robber who's breaking into your house for an ID, right? Both kinds have weapons and both are hungry. And a hungry person is nothing but a hungry person until they have eaten. So when they came and demanded eggs, bread, vodka, money, shoes, jackets, no one thought of them as "defenders"; people were afraid of having their throats cut as a parting gesture. And for providing that kind of "help" the Germans would take revenge and shoot down entire families, entire villages. Because only they had the right to requisition goods from the peasants. And the German reprisals in turn led to retaliation from the partisans, the real ones, who took their revenge on the Germans by attacking a village of settlers, for example, killing the "ethnic Germans" and confiscating their inventory. Then the Germans would strike back in turn with a punitive expedition and send a whole Polish village up in smoke. A crazy cycle of cause-and-effect. The people in the villages were threatened from all sides and robbed in all possible ways, because they provided the first link in the food chain.

Against this backdrop, is it any wonder that people were wary of helping strangers? When you could get killed for feeding "bandits" … And yet there were those who did open a window …

*

Opening a door, on the other hand, was a different matter. In occupied Poland the punishment for harboring Jews, for instance, was severe: the whole household would either be shot on the spot, along with the Jews being hidden, or else all would be send to a camp. So, very often, the door didn't open.

Nor did it open elsewhere. Anti-Semitism in the 1940s was a pandemic disease. Even outside Nazi Germany it was institutionalized and state-sponsored in countries like Romania, Hungary ... and Vichy France. (In contrast to, say, the Polish government-in-exile, which sponsored resistance to the German occupation and repeatedly urged the Allies to take action to stop the mass killing of Polish Jews.) Of course, even when there could have been some possibility of escape, the doors in the West remained closed to refugees seeking asylum ...

Children always pose a problem

Children always pose a problem. You can go about killing fathers and mothers in the normal way, but what about the children? Because what can you really charge them with outright? Even inventing something plausible is out of the question. What can a two-year-old be accused of? Can you say she's your enemy? Or that he has accomplices? Is a saboteur? A partisan? That she's acting to subvert the state? That's laughable. None of the usual political hypocrisies apply. A child is like an alien who doesn't know on what planet he or she is living, who has just appeared and doesn't understand anything yet ... It took some time before a few individual sadists—for example from the ss—showed the regular soldiers of the Wehrmacht that it is possible and even necessary to kill the little ones, and that pretexts are neither required nor expected.

*

Events such as what happened in Bila Tserkva in Ukraine comes to mind ... which I saw in a film about the history of the Wehrmacht (from a pack of DVDs I bought at the local flea market). In August 1941 the ss shot eight hundred Jews from that town. Standard procedure: bullet to the back of the neck, over a pit. The man responsible for the operational-logistical support was Field Marshal Walther von Reichenau, commander of the Wehrmacht's 6th Army. A nice older gentleman. The documentary clips show him sharing a sandwich with a common soldier.

The murdered Jews had children who had not been shot. Ninety boys and girls, or perhaps a few more. The oldest was seven. And what about those who were thirteen? Fourteen? Fifteen? Good question. They had already died, as adults. Good answer. According to the film, the children were locked inside a school, and sat there quietly. No, most of them cried. On the floor, in rags, some naked. In their own waste, dirty diapers, an unbelievable stench. How long did they stay there? Did anyone feed them? That's unclear. The film doesn't show them being torn from their mothers. Did the children think their mothers were coming back for them? Children don't believe in the future: *now* for them is always. The officer to whom the problem was referred was named Helmuth Groscurth. He had a high forehead, glasses, almost looked like a doctor. It's possible he stood at the threshold of first one room and then another, all in a dither as he stared at the children crawling, sitting, standing, walking ... Groscurth— who had been known to protest crimes committed by the ss—pursued the matter all the way up to Field Marshal von Reichenau.

At last the field marshal answered: "As a matter of principle, I decided that, once begun, the operation should be carried out expediently." Von Reichenau was clearly a man of character.

The children in Bila Tserkva stopped crying.

And Lt. Col. Groscurth filed his report: "Measures have been taken against women and children that are no different from the atrocities of the enemy." Although his main objection there seemed to be the effect on the morale of the German soldiers.

The film doesn't say how the children were killed. But it should, because it's important. For a documentary, the film is extraordinarily polite, and gives a highly simplified picture of the Wehrmacht's crime.

"Well," the decent soldiers will say in later years, "in every unit there are always a few rotten bastards." So … among the ten million who served on the Eastern Front, that would be about five thousand rotten bastards … at least those are the estimates for the Wehrmacht. That's probably not so many … But those aren't the complete figures; the Waffen-ss ought to be included as well, and there the percentage of rotten bastards was undoubtedly significantly higher.

*

"In every unit there are always a few rotten bastards …"

One Wehrmacht captain—where was it, Serbia or Russia? It was Serbia. In any case definitely not Western Europe. So, this captain had invited a farmer and his wife over to his place ("his place"—in their country). He wanted to ask them something, but he got annoyed because they were talking over each other, because their children were screaming, and besides why even bother? So he gave up asking whatever he was going to and decided to shoot the father. Silence. Next he shot the mother. Another silence. A little girl and boy were left. The boy was about ten, the girl a little younger—about the same age you were back then. And there was an infant as well. A bullet to the back of the boy's neck, just outside the door, and the matter was quieted further. The little girl, her eyes open wide—and then came some real noise … Another shot—and the eyes closed. Finally, only the infant was left, practically a newborn, now nobody's. The baby cried the way babies do, without understanding, simply from living. "Take that animal away," the captain shouted, and grabbed the thing by its legs and tossed it out into the snow.

"As a rule we didn't do those kind of things," the horrified Wehrmacht generals whispered to each other at Trent Park in England, where they were interned beginning in 1942. They were housed in a beautiful country residence, in single rooms; they played billiards, drank brandy by the fireplace, and waited for the end of the war and the military tribune. They drank brandy by the fireplace, lit cigars, read books, watched films, took walks, and had clothes stitched by a London tailor who came every two weeks to take their measurements ... Meanwhile they drank brandy by the fireplace and told one another this and that about the fronts where they had been fighting. This and that about millions of victims. What they didn't know was that every one of their rooms was bugged; after all, in paradise one ceases to be vigilant. Until recently a hundred thousand pages of transcripts from these recordings were discreetly locked up in the British archives, hidden from the rest of humanity ...

All the officers there came out unscathed. A few minor obstacles, some phony verdicts, mandated moments of reflection ... History likes to frighten its generals, but it is reluctant to punish people who might be of further use, isn't that right? Justice, on the other hand, can be found in the dictionary under the letter *J*.

*

And did you know, Mama, that the Wehrmacht *Soldbuch*—the soldiers' paybooks—contained a list of ten commandments for waging war—a significant testament to "human and civic conscience"? For instance, the first commandment: "The German soldier will fight honorably for the victory of his people. He would dishonor himself by resorting to cruel deeds and unnecessary destruction."

Reading on, the soldier could find further noble guidelines, for instance, that no enemy who gives himself up should be shot (including partisans and spies); that prisoners of war should not be mistreated, and that nothing should be taken from them except weapons and maps; that dum-dum bullets are prohibited, that the Red Cross is inviolable, the civilian population is inviolable, that plundering is prohibited as is the willful destruction of historical monuments and buildings that serve the worship of God, the arts, the sciences ...

Ach, tears come to one's eyes ... Where are those handsome boys in uniform, where are those wonderful wars, it's enough to make you want to experience them yourself.

It stands to reason that every soldier received his pay, right? And that he had to pick up his *Soldbuch* before handing it to the quartermaster? Because surely something had to be checked off. So the soldier encountered those commandments more than once, more than once his eye slid down that beautiful martial poem ... Yes, that very civilized text was well suited to the *Kulturträgers'* idea of the soldier. Oh well. But in the end it turned out to be the script of a play put on in a military theater, in a production plagued with misfortune.

"Rizaty, rizaty"

"The children weren't supposed to know anything, but they found out. What about you, Mama, what was the worst thing you found out? It was about the Ukrainians, right? Before the fire ..."

"I was standing by the stove listening in on our relatives from Ruszów. They had come to us in Sochy to escape the Ukrainians. They slept on the floor, side by side, since our house wasn't big, but before going to bed they told stories so scary I just froze right there by the stove. Everybody seemed to be in a trance, so much in shock they didn't realize that the children were right there, able to hear everything they were saying. And that they were unintentionally giving these children a picture straight from the bowels of hell. I stood by the stove and my only thought was to hide behind it, hide behind the stove—because I couldn't stand it anymore. The figures huddled in front of me around the kerosene lamp on the table disappeared, and the ones in the darker, unlit corners of the room vanished even more quickly, and instead of shadows on the wall I saw wells full of drowned children, heads split open by axes, hands sawed from arms, eyes gouged, breasts cut off, and I heard those horrible voices: *"vykhodyty, lyakhie mordy"* and *"rizaty, rizaty"*—"come out, you Polish mugs," and "cut them up, cut them up." When the Germans later came to Sochy it was a tragedy, but I was so afraid of those Ukrainians that even today as an old woman I would run away from them, or at least hide behind the stove ..."

"I understand, Mama, but there were also cases where a Ukrainian mother saved a Polish child from the pogrom and didn't hand her over to the killers. For instance, the Zamlicze: when the Ukrainian Stepan Stolarczuk discovered the three-year-old daughter of his murdered Polish neighbors, the Barańskis, on the dung-heap, his wife took the child in, even though she had three of her own. And when the Ukrainians carrying out the massacre came to take the child, she held on to that girl so tightly they couldn't tear her away. They told her to give them the little girl, that they wouldn't do anything to her, that they would just take the girl and toss her across the roof, but she refused to let go, and that went on for a while."

Mama, I'm friends with more than one Ukrainian woman, and I don't want to generalize, let's talk about individual people, individual cases ... For instance, one Ukrainian man saved a neighboring Polish woman along with her child, at risk to himself, while another nailed a person to a door and took such delight in the deed you could see his eyes flashing and the veins popping out on his neck. In the Volhynian village of Kisielin there was a Ukrainian who took his seven children out to the yard and lined them up by size and killed each one, simply because his wife was a Pole. It's impossible to imagine what was going on in his head. And more than one Ukrainian killed the mother of his children if she was Polish; all of a sudden a difference in blood corroded the family ties and everything fell to pieces ...

A terrible year, that 1943, everyone was killing each other—just one month after Sochy was burned down there was the infamous Bloody Sunday in Volhynia, on the 11th of July: hell on earth. They did horrible things to the children. After all, children are only innocent for a little while, right? That logic is hard to refute. Guilt merely waits until children grow up and take it on themselves. Should the enemy be allowed to come of age and spawn? The sensible thing is to kill in a bloody rampage, where you kill as though you were deifying yourself—or rather diabolizing. Back then the Ukrainians were desperate for an independent homeland. They would have married the very devil to get what they wanted. And they did. And it was the perfect time for such a match, too. In exchange for their soul, the devil promised to deliver the body of Ukraine into their hands, whole ...

"My God, the things people were reporting then!"

"They said it then, and later they wrote it down so it wouldn't be forgotten, because today no one would believe it."

*

A lot of Ukrainians served in the Waffen-ss. Ukrainians and other adopted Nazis, taken in as Germanic sons of the Reich. Towards the end of the war nearly half of that formation consisted of foreigners. Himmler was a fantasizer who had scientific backing. At the Anatomy Institute at the Reich University in Strasbourg, which had Himmler as its patron, the anatomist August Hirt collected skulls of murdered camp inmates as part of his collaboration with Bruno Beger, a trained anthropologist, who hoped to prove that at some point in the annals of Germanic history a certain amount of Germanic blood had dispersed through the Ukraine and Scandinavia, all the way up to the Baltic states and beyond. Himmler believed this because it enriched his vision of the great ss dominating the European empire. Today only aficionados of that historical period remember that, apart from the Ukrainian, Hungarian, Estonian, French, Swedish, and Norwegian Waffen-ss divisions, there was also a Muslim one—made up of Bosnians who felt that by some historical miracle they were the heirs of Germanic tradition. They had pretty caps to go to war in, too, a kind of Nazi fez ... Hitler himself, however, held them in deep disregard; his racism was crystal-clear. The same applied to the Ukrainians; he disdained them as wild and uncivilized, and the proclamation of an independent Ukraine he considered an act of insolence and ignored. But their murderous rampages directed at Poles and Jews he considered highly useful indeed, from a historical point of view. First the Ukrainians would serve in the devil's kitchen, and then they themselves would become dessert, after the other Slavs had been eaten. If the Ukrainians had known Hitler better, they might have showed more restraint when it came to murdering.

In Sochy the people were terrified of the Germans and deathly afraid of the Ukrainians.

Subhumans in a subvillage

The operation was called a "punitive expedition." The punitive expedition was preceded by a provocation, a show starring two German informers disguised as partisans, who attempted to purchase weapons in the village—and succeeded.

During the occupation the local village leaders would meet every week; the Germans knew that something was going on in Sochy, that the leader there was hosting meetings, that members of the Home Army were coming in from the forest, to get food ... At the time, people tended to keep out of other people's affairs—especially those in other villages—there was too much going on, and the less one knew, the better, but it was obvious to everyone that Stanisław Ferenc, my grandfather's brother, was in touch with the partisans. The leader from Szozdy warned him to watch out so something bad didn't happen. And in the end it did, two men rode up in broad daylight looking to buy weapons. That convinced the Germans that Sochy was a partisan village. Later, the people from the forest killed one of the two men—it turned out he was a *Volksdeutscher*, an ethnic German—masquerading as a Polish partisan.

But to this day the villagers from Sochy don't talk much about that. Those weren't things to talk about then and they aren't now. Peasants are generally restrained, everyone minds their own business, and once they decide to do something they don't parade it about but simply do as they see fit. Besides, who was supposed to preserve the memory of the underground conspiracy since all that was left in the ruins was a cluster of widows and children?

Punishment meant punishment. That's why they didn't deport anyone from Sochy. The villagers came out of their houses carrying their identity papers that no one wanted, and this was already a bad sign. My grandfather went back inside to fetch the can with the money, hoping to ransom his family in case they wound up behind barbed wire in Zwierzyniec. He ended up lying dead on the path. The tin can was lost. All the Germans were after was revenge. At the time, the overall fear of the partisans was very much on the rise; in addition to the usual bands of robbers and wartime hyenas, the Roztocze forests were home to numerous and effective units of the Home Army and the Peasant Battalions, who carried out various anti-German operations, including ambushes on German trucks, on transports of food and fuel, on trains carrying German settlers. Skirmishes on the access roads into the towns and villages usually ended poorly for the Germans, and the black villages lived in constant tension and a state of military alert. And what was bad for the Germans was bad for the Polish peasants. Because of that crazy cycle of reprisal and retaliation. Three days after Sochy was razed, the partisans retaliated by burning down a village of settlers, Siedliska.

*

Fear is a good inducer of crime: in Sochy the Germans wanted to do nothing but kill and burn in order to fear less. And so that they would be feared more. They didn't employ any special method except what was suggested by the topography—the hills surrounding the valley provided ideal placements for machine guns. The yards, the out-buildings, the doors to the homes were clearly visible. And a single road ran straight as a bullet right through the middle of the village.

When I read—or heard—the accounts, I was struck by how sloppy these Germans seemed to be, that they didn't apply themselves with their stereotypical meticulousness. There were several instances where they first only wounded someone, then botched an attempt to finish the person off, and finally just gave up and left him there to die a slow, agonizing death, or else to be burned alive. A shattered jaw or a gouged-out eye, and still alive. And in the meantime they kept on moving and firing; they weren't especially keen about the work, they were just nonchalantly doing their job, killing people the way a cow eats grass. The more I think about it, the more con-vinced I am that there is a better and a worse evil, and that our family was fortunate to draw the better of the evil lots.

That one of them picked up a girl by the hair? So what, since he put her back without smashing her against the wall. Those soldiers went and did what they were sup-posed to—what Globocnik and Himmler ordered. They even acted as though they were bored; every time they turned around it seemed there was another village to burn ... In fact, the operation in Sochy must have come as a relief because for the moment there was no plan of deportation, just plain extermination. Killing to kill time.

It was necessary to punish the subhumans living in the subvillage. Because the village was helping the partisan-bandit-Jews. And anyone who helps the partisan-bandit-Jews is a partisan-bandit-Jew themselves.

My grandfather's brother, in other words my great-uncle, was the village leader, and therefore a public individual, as they say today, and therefore first in line for a bullet to the head: "Sir, I'm not guilty." *Bandit*. Kill him. His brother, Antoni: unmarried. *Bandit*. Kill him. A child: "Sir, what is a child guilty of?" The gun goes off.

A murderous fury? By no means. Cruelty—nothing extraordinary. Even the famous fear of partisans that the German propaganda instilled in the ranks and among the officers from the very first days of the war in September 1939 seems to me in this case to have been tamed or used up, diluted into dull routine. "A job like any other," could be said of the Schupo detachment that arrived to carry out the assignment. And even if one corporal's veins popped out and his face went red as he shouted "Bandits, food! Bandits, vodka!"—it didn't mean much, he probably had that same temperament in everyday life.

However, in Wywłoczka, a smaller village nearby, there was more work to do because there they had to sort the villagers and decide who was fit for what—who to shoot and who to chase off to the camp at Zwierzyniec. Killing and burning are straightforward enough; the rest requires a bit of decision-making. Breaking the commandment "Thou shalt not kill" was easy and even enhanced the feeling of soldierly solidarity during the actual killing and the tedious going from house to house, shooting and finishing people off and setting the buildings on fire. So the work in Sochy was very basic—a military no-brainer. And since airplanes were also part of the plan, half the work took care of itself. I wonder who dreamed up the idea of sending six (or was it nine?) Stukas to attack those few dozen cottages? In that narrow little valley. Some wasteful planner of the "punitive expedition"? Back then they attached little tubes to the bombs so when the plane dove at maximum angle these special sirens would start to scream. Known as trumpets of Jericho, they were designed to instill fear. The Stukas were like the horsemen of the Apocalypse let loose on a village where the houses were made of cards.

The Lublin State Archive possesses a memorandum—a daily report, sent by teletype—from the Headquarters of the German Order Police on June 2, about the pacification of the *Banditenortschaft Sochy*, informing that the village was burned down in a flame-fight with the support of the German air force. The inhabitants were liquidated.

"The military police and special units from Zamość searched the bandit locality of Sochy, twenty-seven kilometers from Zamość. During the fighting the locality caught fire. Air support called into the battle resulted in the annihilation of the village and its inhabitants (*Bevölkerung vernichtet*)."

No blood, nothing but euphemisms, gentle stylistic touches.

This was all reviewed in the 1990s by Władysław Sitkowski from Zwierzyniec, who also happens to be a poet. He somehow became particularly engaged with Sochy. If not for him, everything would have passed away along with the individual people, and hardly any testimony would have survived on paper. He made sure nothing would be lost; he mobilized the survivors and had them recount their stories. He is the author of the collective memory of Sochy. I personally have him to thank that my family album is full of living faces, and that I know the fates of my close relatives and more distant kin. I have no idea why, out of all places, he chose Sochy; perhaps he had family there?

*

See, Mama, how you've become a little girl now. That's from the disease. Once again you have big eyes and a braid. Only now it's gray, and you feel so helpless. And you're not shouting at anybody. Oh, how you sometimes shouted when you were a grown-up! Did you know how afraid of you I was, back when you were my mother? Now it's pleasant to be together, now that I'm grown up and you are small and weak. Now and then I get mad at you, that's normal, the power structure has changed. In certain everyday situations, for instance if you lose a key or repeat some stupid rumor you've heard in the store. I can't believe you actually believe those fairy tales.

Sometimes you even make faces, just like a child. There's this one sly look you used to have when you wanted to know where the chocolates were—knowing, of course, you weren't supposed to have any. "What do you want to know for?" I asked. "Because I want to know," you answered, and when you looked at me I saw a little girl: you once upon a time, or maybe myself? It doesn't matter—some little girl who thought no one could guess her intentions ...

When I again become a child, I hope my daughter will have it in her heart to take care of me, but that's hard and something you can't demand. I can see for myself how much patience is needed when parents and children exchange roles. There's also a slight distaste, a strange existential one, because the feelings have changed directions and are now swimming against the current, against the previous course of events.

That time

Every army is a band of executioners on the move. Transformed, inspired, as though from another world, they have license to perform their bloody mission. Contemporary or recent massacres shock us because the horror seems so close that we sense it could happen to us. We no longer naively believe that war is something confined to history because people got smarter. How could activities as attractive as raping women and smashing children against walls possibly be done away with?

"And so it happened, that not only did we hack apart boyars, peasants, and women, but even split infants in two at their mothers' breasts, and that is how it had to be," a Polish man wrote from outside Moscow at the beginning of the seventeenth century. And that's how it's been since the beginning of time … When the cradle of civilization was rocking, and Homer was creating *The Iliad*, what words did he put in the mouth of Agamemnon? A command that the soldiers not spare children in their mothers' wombs. ("Let us not spare a single one of them—not even the child unborn and in its mother's womb.") When THAT TIME comes, there is no "have mercy" …

*

The human soul is not monolithic, extreme situations bring out unexpected aspects, certain savage instincts reveal themselves, the terrible faces of *us/not-us*, a different visage altogether. The Hutus who took part in the killings said it wasn't they who murdered, but a devil inside them. After all, they knew the Tutsi they were killing, because they were their neighbors in the village. Earlier they had sat on benches in front of their houses together and watched the sun go down, drinking and talking. But when THAT TIME came, they had to kill them. They had to tear the pretty Tutsi children to ribbons, cut the round breasts and slender noses of the beautiful Tutsi women, rape them with clubs spiked with nails, spill their guts and drag the fetuses from their wombs. The frenzy of massacre. The euphoria of going beyond the limit. Orgasmic evil. What happened? They don't know—only the devils do ...

*

Occasionally, I think: why go back to that one village, that burned and bombarded Sochy, since there have been thousands of others before and after? Near or far, in Africa or Asia ... For instance, the recent heavy bombing of Tora Bora by American planes. Villagers died there because they were counted among the fighters, just like in the Zamość region. The war propaganda of today works in the same way: the enemy is dehumanized with the consistent use of daily lies, that are repeated with deep conviction by politicians and journalists. The B-52s drop their bombs, tearing clusters of people to pieces. The shock waves crush the internal organs—not only of the possible terrorists, but also of their wives and children, and of those who were housing them. Roofs fly off and houses are turned to ashes. Just like in Sochy. In the twenty-first century, too, people extract the gold teeth from the dead following the massacre: after all, gold is gold, it passes from hand to hand, just like during the German occupation of Poland several decades ago.

The word "Nazism"

Stutthof was worse than Birkenau. Birkenau was worse than Auschwitz. Auschwitz was worse than Dachau and Buchenwald. There are lighter and darker hells, Mama. In one they shoot you in the head, offering you death as a metaphysical moment, which goes by so fast you barely notice; in the other they press death onto a living organism and you howl for hours at the limits of what your body can take, or really you are at the depths of an abyss of pain. Concentration camp survivor and psychiatrist Viktor Frankl writes that all suffering is similar to the behavior of a gas. If a certain quantity of gas is pumped into an empty chamber, it will fill the chamber completely and evenly, no matter how big the chamber. That's an important sentence, a key thought, which at first I couldn't agree with but later had to accept. Because whether you have a toothache or your leg has been torn off, whether your child died or your humanity has been amputated—you are a figure of pain and there's no room for anything else.

Mama, you don't like to speak of *Nazis* because that word sends things into the heaven of abstraction. Or into the hell, of course. In any case, the specific criminal van ishes from sight as the word *Nazism* absolves individuals of their guilt.

The intellectual Jean Améry—who was Austrian by birth, French by choice, and Jewish by fate—was tortured by the Nazis and then sent to Auschwitz. "It wasn't National Socialism that was beating me, it was Lieutenant

Praust with his accomplices," he writes in *At the Mind's Limits*. He, too, didn't like the term Nazism because it doesn't have a face, only emblems and a uniform. And it wasn't the uniform that dislocated his shoulder and it wasn't the emblems that tortured him, but Lieutenant Artur Praust, someone with a concrete name, born in … related to … working at … In this case working with the Gestapo—and the work assigned to Praust was suited to his temperament, well-matched with his skill set, we might say today. So it wasn't National Socialism in the torture room, but Praust: a short Gestapo man with a hoarse voice and a Berlin accent, over fifty, who tormented a thirty-year-old writer from Vienna. Did anyone sentence that Praust after the war? What happened to him, anyway? No one knows, he dissolved into the sea of Nazism … Meanwhile Améry stayed a broken man; in the end he couldn't bear his life, he committed suicide, just like our countryman Tadeusz Borowski, another writer and former prisoner in Auschwitz … Sometimes trauma keeps forcing life back to the same point in time, causing that moment to never pass, no matter what you do to overcome it, writing books included.

The burned-out valley

The planes flew in. They dropped their bombs, then strafed with machine guns. A first, a second, a third plane descended with a frightening howl, so low the fuselage practically grazed the rye that was flattened by downwash, while the machine guns ripped apart bodies both living and dead. I asked my uncle Jaś what he remembers. He remembers airplanes flying as if they were practicing maneuvers; they came from the airstrip outside Zamość. He remembers how a chimney collapsed when they fired at it. Jaś stopped his ears because of the noise; he hadn't known anything could be so loud. After all, back then the villages had neither tractors nor buzz saws, and since the war broke out no one even had radios at home. The only audible sounds were people talking, or animal voices, or at most a thunderstorm. But that roar of airplanes flying just above the ground, it was like thunder that didn't fade but came closer and closer and louder and louder until it solidified into a giant rock of sound.

It may have been after 11 a.m. when the planes flew away. And the silence fell. The few people who had survived were lying down. The children didn't cry, the wounded didn't groan, because the silence was stronger—so strong no one made a peep. At last they began to get up, carefully, because they were afraid what world would meet their eyes. First they looked into the sky—empty. Then they looked all around—and didn't recognize what they saw. Because how could they recognize something from nothing? Because nothing was left, the valley was burned out, and the charred beams were still smoldering down below, amid the few chimneys that had remained standing.

Only then did a single wail, a single shout escape from the mouths of the survivors.

*

"But you know, Mama, those planes were a lucky thing. If they hadn't planned to send in the bombers, the Germans would have had a lot more time and would have killed absolutely everyone, there's no doubt they would have been more accurate, more cruel. There were so many pretty girls in Sochy: surely they would have raped more than one. They would have dared to do more than kill and burn, as they did in other villages. Especially since this time they weren't deporting people or sending them to work in the Reich. Their task was to punish, and punishment offers many interesting possibilities ..."

"I remember a goat, walking in the orchard."

"The goat survived? How was that?"

"I have no idea, it was grazing, Grandfather's orchard didn't burn down. Aunt Anastazja found the goat and milked it. She had a little glass, very small, two spoonsful, probably for vodka. One by one she offered each of the children milk to drink. When it was my turn I tried, but I couldn't swallow, because my throat was like stone. I spit it out. I gave back the glass. There are a lot of children, she said to me, I can't manage it all, you have to go to Tereszpol. In Tereszpol we still had relatives—Uncle Michał who later moved to Malbork, and others, too, including someone named Jagusia, she wasn't married. I can't remember anymore."

*

You didn't answer her because you couldn't, since your throat was clamped shut. The four of you left—there was also Tadek, Anastazja's son; he carried Kropka. You knew the way because you'd taken that route to the church in Tereszpol for catechism class. It was seven kilometers away, through Szozdy.

*

"We walked towards Szozdy, heading for Tereszpol, through the village that was still burning, or rather through what was left of the village, because there were only beams lying around, still smoldering; now and then something fell and we didn't know from where. We passed bodies lying among those burning beams. Many bodies, big and small, none of them looked like anyone we knew. We stared at those corpses and they all seemed foreign, lying there in this wasteland—where did it all come from?"

"Jaś told me that at some moment he had to walk past a dead child. And next to the child was a burning beam. And that child was such a sight that Jaś was more afraid of it than of the fire. 'I don't know who it was, whose child it was,' he said, 'but I tried to place my legs so as not to touch him and at the same time not burn myself on that beam, because I was barefoot. It was a miracle I managed to pass between them.' For many years he would dream about that scene, and wake up with a shout. It wasn't the death of his parents or the fire that burned down the whole village, but that child and the burning beam, and the fact that he had to pass by them. After that you all left the road and took the paths across the fields. When you came near Szozdy you saw Germans regrouping after the operation."

"I don't remember that …"

"They were already climbing onto the trucks, returning to their unit, it was time for their midday meal. You hid in the woods. You don't remember that? Jaś told me about it. By the way, would they have shot you? Maybe. Back then you were sure they would have. As soon as they drove off you got up and hurried on to Tereszpol. All very quietly, without words, as if something was guiding you, something that knew what to do. And that Tadek, how old was he?"

"Fourteen? I think that's right."

"He led you and didn't have to say a thing. And in Tereszpol do you remember where you went?"

"To the priest's house. They sat us down at the table and gave us each a slice of bread with lard. But I couldn't swallow anything."

"Because of the throat."

"No doubt because of that. The grown-ups talked among themselves. Every now and then I caught a sentence like 'the lady with the withered hand, the one who works in the parish office, she'll take the youngest one to raise at home.'"

"Who said that?"

"I don't know who, but Kropka held onto me so tight and wouldn't let go, like a cat digging in its claws. Then I managed to say no. That I wasn't going to give Kropka to anyone. And we waited for our Mielnik grandparents to come from Stolnikowizna. After all, they were bound to come for us. They'll take us. So they took us to that Jagusia's place and we slept in the hayloft."

"Who was that Jagusia?"

"I don't remember. She was young. Maybe a relative. We

were there two weeks, more or less. They didn't take us to the funeral of the village. Not even me. I heard them downstairs in the kitchen saying we can't take her, she's still in shock, she's barely speaking. When they came back I heard people say that when they buried our parents, blood was trickling out of the coffin. They had a coffin because in Szozdy there was an honest acquaintance who owed my father something, and to pay off the debt he arranged for a coffin. He could no longer pay back the money, but he made a coffin big enough for two or else he had it made. And Mama and Papa were buried in it together."

"How is it possible that blood was trickling? It was two or three days later, because by the time they took everyone, by the time they dug out ..."

"I don't know, but that's what people said. That's what happened."

"There may have been an internal hemorrhage. That can happen when lots of blood collects in one spot and the body is jolted or turned. If your father was shot in the right side, the bullet must have hit the liver, which is full of blood ... And your mother, where was she wounded, because you never told me and I ought to know: where did that German shoot her?"

"In the mouth."

*

In Tereszpol you waited two weeks for your grandparents to come from Stolnikowizna. Because by the time someone went there with the news of the tragedy—since there were no radios or newspapers—by the time they found out that Józia's children didn't have anyone to take care of them ... Well, it was forty kilometers and the only transportation was horse or bicycle. Of course, the Germans had trucks and motorcycles; those were short distances for them.

*

Helena and Józef, your mother's parents. Grandfather Józef Mielnik was the one with the flaxen mustache which he twirled upward. Grandfather Józef Ferenc was the one with the black whiskers that never turned gray. Your Mielnik grandparents borrowed a wagon and rode to Tereszpol to fetch you. They put you in that wagon and went back to Sochy, to see the house that had burned down and the basement that had survived. And what was left in that basement.

There were pillows, browned from the heat. One was worth taking, but smelled strongly of smoke … That pillow stayed intact until your wedding, your grandmother gave it to you as your only dowry … And your father's bicycle survived. Later your mother's brother Władek would ride it. And your father's sheepskin coat was also good for him. And a watch, a very decent one, silver, with a chain—Władek also inherited that. Afterwards when he rode around with you perched on the frame of that bike, he would always say, "This is your papa's bike." And when you looked at the watch with the chain he would say, "This is your papa's watch." As though to justify how he wound up with those things … Or maybe he was simply speaking honestly to a little girl? There was also that tin box with money hidden in the basement … What ever became of it? You don't know.

They put everything on the wagon and set off.

The crying curse

Children are unable to express their emotions in speech. They don't yet know the healing power of words. They flounder about in despair, suffocate with fear, choke with tears; their psychic life is more elemental than that of adults, who already have some points of comparison, some larger universe. Children have a limited capacity of recognition, and when that space is filled with oppression it's as though the child were constricted by an iron band—from which there is no escape.

*

"You cried every day for a year, for hours on end. It was impossible to stop, as though you were under a curse. That a human being, and a child at that, could have so many tears? Where do they come from?"

"It was enough to tilt my head and they would pour out from my eyes, as if a vessel inside had been overfilled, and some inexhaustible source kept supplying the sobs from within. To the point that it started to damage my eyes. I don't mean the swelling and turning red—that was normal, but I was losing my sight. First everything started rocking back and forth, next I started seeing double, and then everything was blurry. I couldn't read."

"But you must have taken a break from the crying, you must have eaten something, gone somewhere."

"I didn't eat much, besides there wasn't much to eat. I did go out—for food. With a little basket, from door to door, without a word. I would stand on the threshold—the people knew what I was after. They would put something in my basket, a potato, a piece of bread, if they had something to give ... I didn't say anything, but when I went like that through the village, I cried even harder, because when I passed between the houses where other children were living with their mothers and fathers who were alive, I felt like crying even more. When it got dark, I would walk back to the bend in the road—that's where my grandparents' house was in Stolnikowizna—and on each side of the street I could see the lamps in the windows and inside I could see figures moving around, big and little. Then the sobbing would come in waves that washed over those windows with all those mothers and fathers. If I didn't cry I would probably have choked on the sobs. Until my grandmother told me that I would go blind if I didn't stop. That's when I must have learned to stop crying and to use my words. One time I came home, set the little basket on the table and started talking. I said that I wasn't going to go begging at the houses anymore. I kept talking, saying the same thing over and over, Grandmother, it's so embarrassing, I'm so embarrassed, I can't stand it anymore. And I didn't burst into tears. The words took hold of me."

"Why did that grandmother send you to go begging in the village?"

"There wasn't anything to eat. A cold stove in the morning and empty pots was our daily reality. There was a lot of hunger then, people were waiting for spring, the first grass, lamb's quarters ... And there were the partisans, more and more of them, they also got their food from the villages, at times by force.

*

I read that Hans Frank introduced a "state of exception" from August through November 1942 "for the protection of the harvest" (for the Reich). Anyone who failed to provide the requisitioned goods, or who slaughtered animals illegally, or incurred any other infraction would receive the death penalty, to be carried out immediately. And feeding partisans was stealing from the Reich. The size of the requisitions was increased every year, and encompassed more and more products. Remuneration, if there was any, was below cost, often it was paid with vodka. Kropka began clawing out little bits of whitewash from the wall and eating that. She also ate little pieces of coal from beneath the stove, putting them into her mouth and sucking on them like candy. As the youngest of the siblings, born during the war, she was never adequately nourished. And after Sochy was pacified she didn't have a mother who would look after her ... Kropka never grew tall, she's the smallest one of you.

Those who still had a cow or a hen were lucky. Grandmother Mielnik didn't have anything except the three of you, who just dropped from the sky, together, one could say, with the ashes of her daughter Józia's burned-down house ... But, still, things weren't as bad as a little further away, in Belarus, where the children were swollen with hunger, the parents were on the front or with the partisans, or killed. Many of those children went wandering along the roads, going from stranger to stranger, winding up in orphanages. "We didn't stroll in the park, we ate it," someone told Svetlana Alexievich in her book *Last Witnesses*. "We ate the young shoots from the pine trees, we nibbled grass ... I know that a man can eat anything." The occupation of Belarus is a forgotten tragedy, like a boat sunk in the sea of the history of the Second World War.

When I was little I used to boast: "My mother's parents were shot by the Germans in the war, what about yours?" Or at the table in kindergarten, when some child would turn her nose up at the "fatty things" floating in the soup, I would say: "You better eat, in the war children would eat anything, even dirt, they were so hungry." Years later I had a more precise picture: that after the pacification children picked baked apples off the burned trees, that they ate sparrows, dogs, cats. In Alexievich's book someone also talks about eating apples like that, after a fire. One of those former girls recalls that during the siege of Leningrad they sold dirt in the marketplace, for eating, from the food warehouses that had burned down. Flavored with sunflower oil or preserves—five flavors of dirt ... That girl—at the time she was twelve or thirteen years old—says that her family could only afford the cheapest dirt, that had been under barrels with herring. It smelled of salt and fish. A kind of ghastly ersatz ... And meanwhile, when we were little, we didn't want the globs of fat in our soup. We couldn't stand salads, beets, red cabbage. And we swallowed kasha as if it were gravel, with tears.

Having children in time of war is a real stroke of bad luck

So, my childhood was permeated with your war, to such a degree that I didn't want to study. Because to what end? Since another war was bound to come back for us ... It would be the same old story and there was nothing to do to change it. I wrote poems because that was quick and easy and didn't require a lot of arduous preparation. I fled German class after three lessons because I couldn't stand the sound of the language. Whenever I heard it I felt anger and fear all at once. I had my dreams, of course—when you're young you live off dreams, but I never made plans for anything beyond summer vacation—it simply wasn't worth it. Because what if a war broke out right after vacation? It's happened before ... Better write poems and do it quickly. The history of literature shows that they will outlast the war; "the song lives on unscathed" as Mickiewicz wrote. Baczyński was my favorite poet. Perhaps I became a poet because I didn't believe in the future? I'm actually surprised I passed my high school exams since I always waited until the last minute to study, because I wasn't motivated to do so any earlier. I didn't see the point; the goal was too far away to change my constant perception that everything was transient, that nothing was guaranteed to last.

And then there were all those moves: new towns, new apartments, new schools, new colleagues, teachers, neighbors, ties broken and made, broken and made ... It was very exhausting, because the constant stimulation of newness can be as exhausting and depleting as a narcotic.

Life without roots. What was it that chased you and Papa all across Poland? If you plotted all your moves on the map, do you know how many zigzags would appear? Katowice—Rybnik—Kołobrzeg—Wrocław—Sopot. It would look like a child's scribbles ... To this day I can't stay put, I'm still moving from one place to another, except no longer with you. From Sopot back to Wrocław, then Warsaw, from there to Gdynia, briefly to Gdańsk then back to Warsaw, where I've had three separate addresses ... If I can't change the city, I can at least change the house; on average I sell my apartment every four years and buy or rent another, even if it's just two streets away ... Without catching my breath. That ease of losing everything, that difficulty of staying in one place, as though I didn't trust the surroundings, escape, escape ... I learned that from you in my childhood and now I can't do otherwise.

*

I've thought about the war for as long as I can remember. I've lived within its context since childhood. I ate because later there might be hunger. I slept, praising the nights that passed without fear. I didn't aspire to live: I merely wanted to survive. A subtle but fundamental difference—and one that determines one's relationship to one's own existence. Hurry up, don't lose any time, don't distract yourself with silly things. Fun isn't very fun, pleasure devours its own tail, every day may be your last, so it's not worth making plans. Somehow you have to wiggle your way through. I experienced love against a background vision of everything coming to a violent end, and was grateful that I managed to. With my first kiss, my first lovemaking. And with becoming a mother right away. I wanted to have only girls because sons go to war.

No, it's better to have boys because girls get raped and killed. So what should I wish for to be safe? I'm laughing. Right here is the wall. And behind the wall—terror.

Then, when I had little children and they declared martial law, I became obsessed with evacuation. Because the Russians might come, right? And then it would be easy for the Germans to come from East Germany. Because Wrocław is their Breslau. My God—and to think our house had once been a German home! And the Russians showed up there in the end as well. They lit a fire on the porch and drank grain alcohol. To this day the floorboards behind the piano are black. That was in 1945; they shot up the plaster outside and went in. They were looking for ss-men, because it was an ss villa. They banged on the piano keys with bottles, making horrible sounds. In the dining room they shot three chandelier shades one by one. They burned the floor on the porch. Broke the glass panes in the china cabinet. They raped a twelve-year-old German girl who was still living there and then tossed her into the basement well. Her mother jumped off the balcony with the younger daughter, right onto the spot where the forsythia is growing today. They ran away through the gardens. Then further and further. Until they stopped somewhere in Argentina or Brazil. I wrote about that once ...

That was my constant frame of mind, the conviction that if the Russians weren't searching for Germans, the Germans would be looking for Russians on our Polish lands, that we were simply in the way, so they would run us off, sweep us away. Two sleepless nights was all it took—and that's easy enough when you have children—for the history of the house where I was living to come back and for me to start breathing the "wartime" air. Whenever I'm afraid I feel it on my body, as though needles were stabbing my temples and cheeks. A sudden, quick pricking; very unpleasant.

I would open the wardrobe and make an escape plan in case of emergency. What was necessary to pack and what could be left behind. Whether the older child could walk on her own or if a stroller is needed; do I carry the smaller child in my arms or do I need my hands free? Food, just in case. How much powdered milk can I carry, how much baby food? A heater for the bottles? That doesn't make sense, there won't be electricity, a thermos is better. Shoes for me, they need to be flat, and pants instead of a skirt so I can run fast. Not to forget the thermometer. And aspirin, of course. Best stow everything in the backpack, the one with the frame, with the name *Mazury* stitched on; it's in the attic. How will I manage? Because Paweł won't be there, he never is when he's really needed, he's that kind of husband. He'd call at the last minute to say he has to help the family of a colleague at work. I would stand in front of the open wardrobe, stuffed top to bottom with the children's things, and fear would go galloping across my deserted soul, and those needles would sting my face. And what if I lose a child? What if someone snatches one away from me? That would be the worst. The very thought made me feel as though I'd grown a coat of ice.

If someone takes a child from a mother, she wants with all her might to die, because the pain is unbearable, but at the same time she wants with all her might to live so that she can save the child. It's a soul-crushing paradox. The child is an anatomical part of the mother, so it's like amputation without anesthetic. I don't think any man is capable of feeling that. He'd have to find some analogy to compare his experience. Maybe it would help to recall a time when he refused to leave his mother's side and squeezed her skirt so tight with his little fist that if someone tried to pull him away it would probably tear the fabric. Except that only happens in the very early stage of childhood, and few people remember. That's why it's so much easier for men to go to war, because they don't bear children, and they don't remember those earliest scenes.

Happily, those attacks of my war-neurosis abated when I had a chance to sleep. After a good night's rest I would get up and feel normal—the rift in my imagination that had let in the icy fear would be repaired. And I would once again be able to live a little.

*

Having children in time of war is a real stroke of bad luck. How many fathers, how many mothers secretly regretted that they had a child right before the war, and—even more foolishly—during it! Fleeing with a child is horribly inconvenient. Sitting with a child in a basement, with enemy soldiers all around—it's frightening. Because she'll squeal, or cry—and everyone will get shot. It's extremely easy to perish because of a child. If a child is hungry you can't explain that he has to wait. And what if she gets sick? There's neither doctor nor medicine, and all you can do is look on as they die ...

For times of war, there shouldn't be any children. They should stay in an all-day preschool the whole war long, behind some kind of colorful wire, behind walls of fairytale thickness, best of all on some other planet. And wait. And afterwards people would come to fetch them, little by little ... How much easier would wars be without worrying about children? Fear for their safety is like a highly toxic gas. It's enough to go crazy. More than one mother did. And more than one mother, in that poisonous fear, suffocated her child.

*

A child who loses her mother during a war can go gray ...
I read in Alexievich about a Belarussian girl who missed
her train because she was picking cornflowers when the
train stopped in the middle of a field. Meanwhile her
mother, her sister, and her entire life was aboard that
train, and that train rode away to some unknown destination. They'd been displaced by the war, evacuated. The
little girl went running after the train carrying her bou-
quet, but the train was going faster and faster. What absolute horror: she's running and the earth is collapsing
behind her. If not for a Red Army soldier who jumped
after her and managed to catch her and shove her onto the
car, she would have stayed there. That night her hair
turned, and by the morning it was completely gray.

I'm surprised that didn't happen to you in Sochy, and
there may have been more reason for your hair to go gray.
You're strong. But you did cry for a whole year.

*

A child being taken from his mother encounters a limit,
an extreme state. And children shouldn't be allowed to
come close to such extremes if they are to develop into
healthy people without disorders. So what can be said
about a generation that spent its childhood in a war? For
instance, yourself. You were nine years old and experienced an extreme event. "Wake up, Renia," you heard at
dawn. Your mother was completely normal and acted
rationally: "Wake up, Renia," you hear your mother telling you. "We have to get out, the Germans are in the village—do you hear—they're burning houses ... Wake up,
here's your dress." The dress was new, it had just been

sewn. Everything was new—the house had just been built, your little sister had just been born. And it was spring. The flowers around the house were blooming. Your whole life was new and completely aware, with a new, barely used awareness. That life had eyes wide open and saw how your father turned to go back inside to fetch the money that was in the tin, and how he collapsed on the path. It heard your mother shouting that your father was dead. And then it watched as your mother also collapsed and ceased moving. Your dress was mussed up. Your awareness lost sight for a long time. And life was no longer clean and new, and would never be again.

Who thinks about children in those times? That it is not permitted to make them sad, or scared, to take them to the edge and abandon them there? Who stops to think about whether such a child will develop into a healthy person without disorders?

Nobody.

Nobody goes to war and kills no one.

Everybody wants to understand ...

Everybody wants to understand the ss-men and other murderers, uniformed or not. To comprehend the nature of evil. *Unde malum?* Finding the answer seems to be the first step in saving humanity.

By unleashing the war, the Germans provided a horrible, traumatic childhood for Jewish, Slavic, and Romani children in Europe during the 1940s. Some psychohistorians claim it happened because their own childhood was terrible. Controversial scholar Lloyd deMause maintains that human history depends on the relationship between adults and children, that childhood trauma is the drive wheel of war, because trauma is inherited and then passed on to the next generation.

He describes childrearing practices that employ violent means—practices known as poisonous pedagogy—which were particularly prevalent in Germany and Austria. The approach lasted through the 1920s and was sanctioned by mass-produced manuals on how to raise children. The author of one such manual prescribed beating the child until it has stopped crying. Babies were swaddled so tightly they couldn't move, were seldom washed, their heads looked like blue cheese, and they lay in their own filth, often strapped to the cradle. Mothers did not breast-feed (this was particularly out of fashion in Bavaria and Austria), presumably because they found it repulsive. In Bavaria nearly sixty percent of the infants died because the mothers fed them a watery flour-meal pap or else gave them a rag soaked with bread to suck instead of a fully nutritious diet. DeMause cites these statistics and relates that parents frequently strangled their children or drowned them in creeks or latrines. Or even smashed their little heads against something. The remaining children lived with the feeling that their mother or father might kill them at any moment. Richer parents gave their newborns to a nanny—a so-called *Engelmacherin*, or angelmaker, who took care of the job for them. The majority of victims were girls, therefore there were significantly fewer of them than boys, supposedly ...

In 2005 that same scholar gave a speech in Klagenfurt in which he cited other data showing that children were beaten with special "disciplining" rods and straps until their skin broke, until they lost consciousness; that they were punished with starvation, with being locked up in a dark chamber, or placed in an ice-cold bath or on a hot stove. If they happened to vomit or soil their pants they were made to eat it. A painful enema was both a punishment and a normal way of achieving regular "clean" bowel movements, and to do that they would tie the child down with rope. There were special stores where children would be taken to be fitted for the proper size of enema tube. There were also special anti-masturbation cages.

In homes, schools, and educational facilities, rape and child abuse were a daily occurrence for girls and boys alike. The pedophile scandals of today are the vestiges of that behavior. Abandoning children was a popular procedure, with Vienna having one of the highest infant abandonment rates in Europe at the end of the nineteenth century. *Kinderfeindlichkeit*—animosity towards children —was the reigning emotion inside the home, both pitiless and accepted—so deMause explained in his lecture. Hard to believe. My God, can it possibly be true?

Because if something is extended through generations

it becomes second nature. Broken and enslaved in childhood, they broke others and enslaved them, because only then did they find some solace and relief—that was the pattern in which they felt wholly themselves. Genocide, Holocaust—that was unconscious revenge on a mass scale, but a revenge exported from the fatherland and unleashed on others, because, like a punishing parent, the fatherland is both menacing and holy; without it there is no life. It was necessary to identify with it in order to destroy inferior nations (bad children), and at last experience something that would make the perpetrators whole, with fully integrated personalities, in a clean and perfect form. Revenge becomes medicine, albeit a bitter one ... It all makes sense. In other words, hundreds of thousands of perpetrators were disintegrated adult children with undiagnosed and unclassified neural damage, resulting in moderate psychopathy.

And now what?

Who to feel sorry for?

Perhaps God?

*

Everybody wants to understand the ss-men and other murderers. An ss-man snatches a woman's baby and tosses it onto the square, onto a pile of others, turns around and shoots the mother who is one enormous howl, and doesn't feel anything. He repeats that several times until finally he feels jaded. He goes home and watches his wife bustling about. He breathes the aroma of freshly baked cake, smiles at the sight of his boy bouncing on a hobby horse. All his inhumanity and ruthlessness suddenly disappear. Daddy is home. Peace, harmony, everything is in its proper place.

There have been hundreds of attempts to glue together this schizophrenia, but in vain. The "banality of evil" didn't prove correct because evil doesn't appear in complete synchronicity with banality, but rather in rotating shifts. On the first shift, it works in such and such circumstances and gives its all. Then it relaxes and jumps into a different existential sphere. A kind of natural demonization ...

The wife of Rudolf Höss, the commandant of Auschwitz, complained to her husband that he should spend more time with his family instead of working and working ... Their children were dressed in lovely clothes left over from Jews who had been gassed. Second-hand clothes, it might be said ... One ss-man from the camp simply took his son along to work; the boy played on the camp grounds, with a nametag saying he was the son of an ss-man, so he wouldn't be mistaken for a regular child and get shot ...

*

Perhaps the "banality of evil" was found in the fact that such a huge number of Germans answered Hitler's call and thereby gave up the most valuable thing they had— their individual conscience. It was the collectivization of conscience, like the agrarian collectivization in Russia. There they promised the peasants: give up your small plot of land and you will work in one big farm and derive profits from it. An added value will be the joy of community. That communal joy was also created by the Germans. They labored in a common moral field. Consistent to the end.

The Germans weren't the biggest murderers in history, but they did comprise the largest murderous collective of all times. It's well known that a significant portion of the citizens supported Hitler's politics. But perhaps not everyone realizes that the Germans engaged more people in war than at any other time in history. Nineteen million soldiers of the Wehrmacht (some sources suggest lower numbers) and about half a million Waffen-SS. Not to mention all the auxiliary forces. Arithmetically, that is overwhelming. Numbers matter.

It's possible to play with the criteria to come up with a more varied pattern in the matter of genocide ... The internet has posted "rankings" of other countries guilty of perpetrating mass murder. The largest number of victims goes to the USSR; the English won first place in the competition of the most killed in retaliation for one resident (colonial times?), while the USA annihilated the most nations (counting the separate tribes); the Australians liquidated the largest number of languages from the earth (there were hundreds of Aboriginal languages), and the French were the first to murder *en masse* for ideological reasons (in the eighteenth century).

*

War will never die. It will only change uniforms. War takes field trips to other countries. And there are days when the great murderous exertion catches up on sleep, and then its quiet nurses go to work, devising whatever peace would best serve their charge, while polishing their tools. War cleverly defends itself at various conferences, when it talks about new strategies for peace using airplanes and ships. War is our common cause. It fertilizes the earth, revives the soul, spurs progress (*polemos pater panton*). Without it, there would be a lack of voltage, and the lights on earth would go out ...

The wonderful thing about war

The wonderful thing about war is that, all of a sudden, evil, which is not very accessible to the average person during peacetime, burdened as it is with the heavy risk of punishment and social condemnation—becomes legally permissible. What's more, it is even endorsed and rewarded by the state. In wartime the human soul first experiences the collapse of the previous "peacetime" moral scaffolding, and then quickly constructs in its place a new internal setting, following a different directive. I speak of "scaffold" and "setting" to underscore how ephemeral conscience really is, at least where ordinary, "other-directed" citizens are concerned.

During wartime it happens that evil, which is running rampant, wants to be useful: it wants to be a better evil than your run-of-the-mill evil, wants to make a name for itself, leave its mark wherever it can, on human flesh, on human skin; it wants to find fulfillment, systematically and within the majesty of the law, even if that law is satanic. My God, if they had had computers in the war, the Germans would have probably gassed everyone except the Nordics, interplanetary aliens included.

*

But perhaps it's time to give the Germans a break. The Russians, for example, also have an impressive criminal record. As do the Ottoman Turks, who led one and a half million Armenians to death. And Mao Zedong's China, and Pol Pot's Cambodia—the map of the twentienth century is dotted with killing fields.

Let's simply add humanity in its entirety—*Homo sapiens* as a murderous species. I saw a film about a fox farm that was recently made using a hidden camera. One of the scenes shows the workers (veritable executioners) peeling the skin off a living fox. They pull it off the animal's head like a turtleneck sweater. From a living fox. The film was two hours long and showed various farms and slaughterhouses in various countries: that scene was one of several that surpassed my psychological limit. I never saw anything more terrifying.

Of course, I wasn't in the war. But for centuries, millennia, humans have been waging war against nature, placing themselves in opposition to, or rather above it.

"Do you remember that a kilometer away from where you lived in Sopot there was a fox farm in the middle of the woods? Don't you remember the stench? Once I went on a walk there with our dog. I was eighteen or even younger. I was passing by that farm when the gate opened and a tractor drove out hauling a trailer. The trailer was full of red bloody pelts. Before my mind worked out what it was I had no way of placing that image. The trailer passed a meter away from me, bumping along on the uneven road. Everything was at eye-level. And then I realized that what I was looking at was a pile of skinned foxes. I stood there paralyzed. And there, in broad daylight, hell took the wrong road and went passing right before my eyes …

"That little Edek Markowicz—I told you that a German soldier had lifted and carried him, just like happened to you—that Edek has another memory from childhood, about how people in the village butchered animals in the slaughterhouse for the requisitioned livestock. He says he looked on as they smashed a bull with the butts of their axes. The animal let out a pitiful roar, but did not cave in. Finally they hobbled its legs, knocked it over, and cut its head off with a scythe. The same villagers who were later shot at by the German army during a deportation ... Edek is now an old man, he's remembered that image his whole life, along with the pit full of children's bodies, and a hunger that was stronger than fear.

"On and on it goes, a neverending extermination—skinned foxes, live cows pulled by their legs onto carousel-like platforms to be slaughtered, chickens whose beaks and claws are chopped off while still alive, as though they had no nervous system but were made from some abstract edible mass. A mass that unfortunately cackled, howled, squealed, kicked. As though these weren't concrete living beings but merely instant meat."

"Stop it."

But these are also pictures of our civilization, snapshots from the thousand-year war. We don't want to see or hear it. And by extension the killing of people, too, will never stop. Because if nobody (apart from a handful of eco-crackpots) is concerned about locking up little calves in solitary cement graves with no light (the supermodern method for producing particularly delicate meat), from where they are taken to be slaughtered after a few months, then why should we necessarily be moved by the killing of children—of an inferior race or enemy nation, or simply the brood of some nasty neighbors? It's always possible to find people for hire who will toss living pigs into boiling water (which of course is against the proper procedure). And it's always possible to find people willing to impale infants on fence pickets, as happened in a few villages during the occupation (clearly not part of the official order). And the bigger children walked by and they witnessed that. Those were the images that were etched in the memory of the survivors.

Cruelty passes from the farm to the concentration camp without major difficulty. It's just a matter of changing the procedure and what goods are named on the invoice.

Of course, I have to repeat: not everyone is capable of murdering children, and not all children are murdered.

But a sufficient number of one group can take a large number and ...

Strapping boys in uniform

Before the war, people were smaller than we are today. And the people from the countryside in Eastern Poland were small even for those times. Meanwhile, the German soldiers—they were strapping boys, specially chosen. The Waffen-ss required a minimum height of 174 cm and their recruits weren't allowed to have even a single tooth filling. The Wehrmacht had fewer restrictions; slightly smaller men could also wear the uniform. Only towards the end of the war did they take everyone, including weaklings and the children from the Hitlerjugend, since they needed a strike force on the Eastern Front. Hitler went up and down the ranks patting the tenderfeet on their cheeks, like a physical education coach before a game, rather than an experienced executioner sending those boys to their deaths.

Nevertheless in the first years of the war they still observed the standards. Thus a Polish peasant wearing a linen shirt, and on cold days a sport coat or jacket, was faced with a tall warrior in a broad-shouldered uniform tied with a leather belt and a buckle claiming divine support. So what if a few years earlier that same soldier might have been treated as a dunderhead in his native village, someone who was always kicked in his behind by his schoolmates, a boy his father beat with a metal-tipped leather strap: in that situation he was master, a hero, an Übermensch—and that was plain to see. Even my thirty-three-year-old grandfather, who had broad shoulders and a strong jaw, must have seemed puny compared to such a superman—especially with his linen shirt and bare head. A "civilian," how does that sound? ... Because "peasant" sounds worse. A subhuman from a subvillage, a thing that practically begs to be shot.

*

Burning down a little village like Sochy was nothing. Wooden cottages with thatch roofs—what's that? A few dirty, simple subhumans that need to be removed, vermin from the East. A similar argument was effective in Rwanda half a century later, only there the people being called vermin by the Hutus were the Tutsi ... But vermin are vermin, anyone can get labeled that way, if the propaganda so chooses ...

Sochy wasn't a rich village, not like Oradour-sur-Glane or Lidice, where the sidewalks were paved. But I did find pictures of a village in the Lublin region where the streets and sidewalks were paved with stone (that village also went up in smoke). Presumably it was easier for the German soldiers to set the thatched cottages on fire, because they didn't consider them proper buildings. Just like they didn't consider poor people in humble clothing proper humans. It's a lot easier to shoot at beings who can be defined differently than the ones doing the shooting. And their definition of Slavs was learned in their schools, so they had everything sorted out. The hierarchy was set forth with amazing specificity, and the Slavs were by no means at the bottom of the ladder. That place, of course, was occupied by the Jews—all Jews, en masse. Intellectuals and tailors, musicians and rabbis, beautiful women and dirty beggars. For them there was actually no rung on that ladder of humanity: they were merely fertilizer for the earth.

*

There's a scene in Elem Klimov's frightening film *Come and See*, based on events that occurred in a poor Belarussian village, events so true they seem like fiction ... A tall, young, and beautifully proportioned ss-man—who looks like Barbie's Ken—tells the villagers who have been locked inside a wooden building where they're about to be burned alive, and who are therefore screaming with fear, that if they leave the children inside they will be allowed to leave. "Whoever doesn't have children may leave through the window. Leave the children." At that moment the screaming grows even more intense.

Later, after everyone has been burned, when the partisans arrive and have to retaliate by killing those Germans (and their Belarussian collaborators), that handsome ss-man says, in accord with his youthful ideology: "Everything begins with children. You shouldn't exist."

*

The case of Agamemnon? A child may always turn out to be the beginning of an unwanted sequel, as the more intelligent warriors are well aware.

Good parents, bad parents

Who would I be if not for those Germans? Would I have inherited my grandparents' house? Would I have a store with orangeade? A father who came from nearby and not from Pomerania? Would I be a teacher in a village school with no time for writing books? I certainly wouldn't have written this book. In some sense the Germans are the instigators of my fate, they gave shape and direction to my life, flinging it out of the predetermined orbit of my ancestors. The notion of evil as the absence of good strikes me as the kindhearted invention of a spinster auntie ... Evil can be expansive and creative.

*

Think, mother. You lost good parents. But there are people who lost bad ones. For them, things are somehow worse. Like the daughter of Amon Göth, who was the commandant of the camp in Płaszów—her whole life was ruined. They (meaning we Poles) hanged her father after the war, of course. "He had an easy death," said Helen Jonas-Rosenzweig, one of his near-victims. Göth's daughter Monika didn't love her mother, she was unable to, and the mother in turn committed suicide years later. Monika's daughter became a drug addict. And Monika herself? Lives with a rotting soul, because guilt causes the human soul to decay. She didn't even know her father, had never called him Papa. She was born in 1945, when he was already in prison.

Feeling guilty for crimes committed by one's father—isn't that a strange phenomenon? Strange, but explicable: genes are immortal, they transmit themselves from body to body and speak to the carrier from the inside, always, without words, informing who we are. And Monika must be carrying Amon Göth inside her. She is tall like her father, so she can be seen from everywhere, though she would prefer to disappear. She hates her very tissue, permeated as they are with the genes of a criminal. She referred to the daughter of another war criminal, Göring, as "that cursed daughter of his ..." And that Edda was such a pretty girl. "I'll never have any pity for the children of criminals," Monika repeats. Which clearly means she has no pity for herself, and that she hates herself, too. She watched *Schindler's List* and for half the film saw her father as though he were alive—smiling, conversing. And every few moments he's killing someone. He stared at Monika from the screen with the eyes of a sad serpent. Mama, the actor Ralph Fiennes was terrifyingly good at suggesting that quality with just his gaze. Imagine that your father appears on the screen as though from the afterlife. And in him you recognize your own gestures, your grimaces, the way you move your body. It's impossible not to feel some connection. Meanwhile, every few moments he's killing someone. The person who contains so much of you. You're bound to hate yourself. And self-hatred is like half-suicide, like being pregnant with your own death. You, too, Mama, carry death inside you, but it is the death of your good parents, a clean business ...

After she turned sixty, Monika wanted to meet Helen. They agreed to meet in Płaszów, on those death fields left over from the camp. Monika, who is tall and thin, towers over Helen, swaying like a reed and trembling ... A wasp flies in from somewhere and buzzes around Helen, and

Monika reflexively shoos it away with her long arms, with a clear affection for Helen, but at the same time as though in slow motion, with no energy. Because is there anything left to salvage? Life is already so tired of that mourning, that penance—it's so tired ...

Monika says goodbye and leaves with a slightly swaying gait, tall like her father, probably a whole head taller than Helen; she walks down the road through the grass growing on the graveyard of Amon's victims. The daughter of a villain, visible from everywhere.

Meanwhile Vivian, the daughter of Helen who was saved, said in the documentary that she has inherited the suffering of her mother, that she is a second-generation victim. And that's what the documentary is called— *Inheritance.* In the film Vivian says that she is able to imagine everything that happened and that she sometimes feels physical pain. That is an innate empathetic connection: the same genes, remembering the experiences of ancestors, and expressing themselves sympathetically. I wouldn't believe it if I didn't experience something similar. Your history, Mama, is sewn into the lining of my life, and I have always felt it like a sharp pair of scissors in my internal pocket.

*

Trauma is inherited in some epigenetic manner. There exists something like an inheritance of acquired traits, though not all scientists are in agreement over this. Some stimulus from the environment effects a change in the appearance or the behavior of a given individual—let's say a fly or a mouse—and that changed trait then appears in later offspring, even though the stimulus has been removed. Research suggests the genes themselves remain unchanged; in other words, no mutation has occurred, but their expression has changed. In addition, the offspring may react to the reappearance of the stimulus even more strongly than the original individual, because of the transmitted aversion.

I, too, would happily disagree, but that genetic expression is stronger than me. I'm thinking of an orphan syndrome I have inherited from you. And my daughter from me. Kropka's son also inherited it from her, and one of Uncle Jaś's daughters had it as well. I was truly sorry to see my seven-month-old girl rocking rhythmically back and forth as soon as she could get on her hands and knees. I used to rock while sitting down, and then on my right side before falling asleep—only on my right side. For thirteen years I couldn't fall asleep without rocking my head on the pillow. After I was told this was bad behavior I did it in secret, patiently waiting for the right moment. Summertime was the hardest, at a children's camp, sometimes a whole hour or more would go by before the children in the room went to sleep. Only then would I fall into the familiar rhythm. I was embarrassed, and at the same time I was otherwise unable to quiet my unease, which came on strongly towards the end of the day. Out of all the colorful happenings throughout the day, something would surface that was dark and empty, deaf and dumb. As if something important was supposed to occur but couldn't. Something that seemed imminent but unable to form, it just lingered there, idle and exhausting, and could only be quieted by rocking back and forth. As a side effect, my hair on the right side was always knotted up and my cheek was more colored. If I had an ear infection, it was only ever on the right side. I was asymmetrical and lopsided, probably psychologically as well. Every tense situation, no matter how slight, set off this particular dynamic which fortunately put me in a fog. I had the same need during the day ... I would lean against a wall and bang my back against it. That was the fastest way to tire myself out, to stun myself calm.

How can it be, Mama? I asked years later, as we observed the way my daughter would act in the early evening; after all, you're the one from the orphanage, not us! You didn't know, and the science then had yet to catch up with the idea of transgenetic inheritance. Meanwhile, the teacher in my little Róża's kindergarten had a different understanding of undesirable behavior in three-year-olds, and one day she was embarrassed to tell me that my child had a habit of rocking on all fours, for instance when another child took away her toy. What has that child gone through, the woman asked in a whisper, over the head of my Róża. Was she perhaps adopted? ... Well, it's true that she comes from being orphaned, completely orphaned, suddenly and totally, in a direct line. That's what I could have answered her, but back then I still adhered to the pedagogic principle that you don't say things in front of children that they don't understand. Particularly because I myself didn't understand where the rocking in the family came from.

Precious little angel

Everyone is amazed to think that Adolf Hitler wasn't born a monster, that at the beginning of his life he might have been a child like any other. Szymborska expressed that same amazement, in line with the prevailing intuition. I'm sure you remember the poem—"Hitler's First Photograph"—with lines such as "Precious little angel, mommy's sunshine, honeybun ..." and:

A little pacifier, diaper, rattle, bib,
our bouncing boy, thank God and knock on wood, is well,
looks just like his folks, like a kitten in a basket,
like the tots in every other family album.

The innocence of that particular child is hard to believe—impossible, in fact: after all, monsters are repulsive from the beginning. For instance, snakes, crocodiles, and scorpions don't spark any affection, even when they are little. They have their destiny written on their faces right away. Hitler, too, should have had some kind of special mark. Something that showed he wasn't innocent, that he wasn't sweet and good, so there would be some justification in not liking him from the start. A human child is not a tabula rasa, as the Enlightenment idealists claimed. They come into the world with a few spots and splotches, even if they were conceived on a crystal table.

That not all children are innocent is well known. I never told anyone about my escapades from my school days in Kołobrzeg. One spring day I skipped school with a classmate who took me along as a companion. She was in a class above me; she may have been eleven. I was in third grade and felt it was a great honor. It wasn't the first time I had cut class, but the first time I had done so completely and left the actual school. We headed out of town, towards Janiska, not too far, one or two kilometers down the asphalt road. We were lured by the former German gardens, now overgrown, the orchard gone wild, the bunkers or earthen basements, the well that was no longer in use because it was "infected" with a drowned fox. It was a place of secret outings for the local children.

I didn't know the girl very well, but I remembered her from youth group rallies; she belonged to a different troop. We went out there and walked around with our sticks, enjoying our freshly won freedom. It was afternoon; green, warm. The unplowed field was dotted with molehills, the earth was breathing. Off to the side was a wet meadow where, during a school outing the previous spring, the boys from class had caught frogs, which they then exploded by blowing them up using straws.

I don't remember the girl's name, or what she looked like, only that she was bigger than me and had straight hair that fell across her face when she bent over a molehill and dug inside with her stick.

She darted from one hill to the next, and I followed. Suddenly she hauled off and started swinging her stick. She called me over and pointed to something in the grass. It was similar to a hamster, only larger. Or to a guinea pig, only smaller. "That's a mole," she said, and hit it again. "It's blind, you know?" I had never seen a mole before; I looked at it with a mixture of fear and curiosity. It was lying on its side, not running away. It was black, with bright paws, like the tiny hands of a doll. And shiny fur. And, indeed, it did not seem to have eyes. "It lives underground and never comes out," the girl explained, and made a disgusted face. "But this one came out," she added. She hit it again and I saw her thick stick striking the little black body, which jumped up like the little bean bags we used for gymnastics. "Moles have to be killed," she said. "They're disgusting." And she went on hitting and hitting, with passion. And as she did she shouted, "You blind thing, you!" And I stood there by her side watching, as though bewitched, not understanding what I was seeing. I didn't say "no," probably because I didn't know if I could. The mole was still moving, but I didn't move. I felt that it was mysterious, unpleasant, bad, but necessary. And maybe I only saw what I saw and that filled me completely, so there wasn't room for any more. When I finally heard her say "It's dead," I felt relief. A dead mole is repulsive, she was right. And that was that. Why did that particular mole come to the surface? It could have stayed underground. Then nothing would have happened. Which one of us said that?

*

I was also a bad girl.

*

Children can be dangerously inventive, in keeping with humanity's general tendencies.

The children in Belarus, for instance, whose parents were killed by the Germans and who were so starved that they ate grass, the leaves of trees, plaster from the walls— these children lost their family ties and with them the ties that connected them to humanity. They transformed into feral beings in a manner that was entirely natural.

Later, when the front came through, they would take stiff, frozen German corpses and ride them downhill like sleds. That only seems demonic: in reality it was simple and pragmatic. The Yakuts in the far north used to make sled runners out of big frozen sturgeon, which they lashed to a seat. There are many known instances where officers ripped open the stomachs of common soldiers to stick their frozen feet inside. I believe that was during Napoleon's march on Moscow. When my orphaned uncle Jaś was chosen to tend the cows in the pasture, he would run out to the field at daybreak, barefoot, onto the field covered with frost, and—undoubtedly like many other clever village children—impatiently wait for one of the animals to defecate, so he could step into the cow patty and warm his feet for as long as possible. That's a simple idea, easy for children to come up with—children and adults alike.

Or the Jewish children in the trains to Treblinka, in which they were transported without food or drink, sometimes for several days, even though it was only a hundred kilometers away from Warsaw—they would lick the sweat off one another. A simple idea. Perhaps they drank their own tears, for as long as they were able to cry.

Object in motion

NKVD and Gestapo: A Blood Brotherhood—that was the name of a documentary recently shown on Polish TV, late at night. At last there is at least partial access to Soviet archives, lifting the red veil of secrecy for the world to see ... and the sights are bloody indeed. For instance, there is documentation of torture and means of killing perfected both by the Bolsheviks and the Nazis, working closely together. They visited each other and exchanged experiences. The mass shooting of enemies of the regime in the Soviet Union, and the liquidation (in concentration camps built on the Soviet model, for example) of anti-fascists and "racial undesirables" in Germany were subjects of consultation. According to the film, the Russians "sold" the Germans the idea of using automobile exhaust as a means of killing, and the Germans later perfected the practice. During the meetings between the NKVD and the Gestapo there was something like today's conference presentations, just without the laser pointers. And they used identical methods for interrogations, as historians from both sides have noted. Only the Nazis were more precise, whereas the Stalinists were more inclined just to have at it. A matter of national temperament.

That tendency was also evident in the games that were played at work. For instance, the idea of killing multiple people with one bullet. In the NKVD prisons before the war, the guards made bets as to who could shoot the most people: they would line the prisoners up close together, naturally taking into account the fire power of a 7.62

caliber. The results varied. Amon Göth, the commandant of the camp at Płaszów, might have heard about that technique before 1939, and if not, it's not particularly hard to come up with such an idea if you have a knack for that kind of sport. From his balcony Amon would practice killing mothers together with the children they were carrying with one shot. So that both fell from the same bullet. It was a test of proficiency. That's not so easy: just try to take down a mother carrying a child, especially when they're moving. The double object is alive and moving, she comes down the path, then turns back, with no idea she's in your sights. And you calmly follow her with your eyes and the barrel of your rifle. You wait until the object is vertically aligned in your sights. The child silhouetted against the mother, like the moon's shadow against the sun during an eclipse. Then *pik* and the target is dead. And if not, if one part needs to be finished off, then the shot was not successful.

Now and then I think about the soldier who shot my grandmother while she was holding Kropka. He shot a woman in the mouth. That's also a technique.

Burnt offering

Before the war all the larger manor houses had a salon with a grand piano, or at least an upright. In other words, somebody there played. Towards the end of the war, in the village Żerosławice, a certain scene took place that seems like something out of a movie but it wasn't. The people who were children there back then remember— in fact, they can't forget it. I read about it in a collection of children's recollections from the war. The Germans shackled forty people and brought them to the manor in Żerosławice, locked them in the barn and in the lofts, and set the whole thing on fire. In the meantime they hauled a piano out of the manor into the middle of the yard. The leader of the executioners sat down at the instrument and played. It was an open-air concert, almost like at Łazienki in Warsaw or Tanglewood in the US, only the scenery was burning. And howling, because it was burning alive: the fire roared, the condemned howled, and the pianist played on. Dance music. Foxtrots. A composition for piano and forty burning voices. A concert the children would never forget ...

Sometimes it only takes a few seconds to burn. One hundred thousand people could evaporate in a single moment. Like in Hiroshima. The Japanese were guilty of horrible war atrocities and were punished for it. They and their children.

Those children survived an apocalypse that no film-maker can simulate, no matter how many special effects might be available. Those children lived a little afterward and recounted what they felt and saw.

Sachiko says, "Since my house was at Togiya, close to where the bomb fell, my mother was turned into white bones before the family altar."

Eleven-year-old Sachiko was five on August 6, 1945. Her mother was likely paying respects to the dead ancestors at the family shrine. On that hellish day and for several days after, many children blundered through the destroyed city all alone, burned and half-conscious, among the ruins and the bloated or charred corpses. Houses were still burning with a bluish-green fire, and the faces of those who were still alive were monstrous and blackened, covered with blisters.

Yoshimi says, "A streetcar was burned and just the skeleton of it was left, and inside the passengers were burned to a cinder. When I saw that I shuddered all over and started to tremble."

Yasuhiro says, "The neighborhood was changed into a melting-pot of terrified confusion. Below the embankment, some children were screaming, crushed under a house. A man who seemed to be their father, although his leg was bleeding rather badly, was trying with all his might to lift the heavy roof, but it didn't move; the children only shrieked more loudly and their father rushed about as if he were insane, shouting to the people passing along the street and asking for help, but not a single person lent him a hand. They were all staggering along like sick people in delirium. I couldn't stand that sight any longer, and turned my eyes toward the river, but it was not the clear stream of the Ohta River that I saw there. Just as if it were all built up, it was filled with houses and dust that had been blown there ..."

Kikukuo says, "I went to the place where mother was and called 'Mother!' But I couldn't hear Mother's voice. I was sad and two or three times I called Mother but no matter how much I called she didn't answer. I fell across her chest and cried and cried. After that, the funeral started. I hated to go away from her side but I had to. As soon as the funeral was over we went to the hospital. For a long time we stayed there. And then one morning when we got up my brother had died. After that, one after another they all died and only my two brothers and I were left ..."

Toshi says, "When Father said, 'Look inside that box,' I opened it and looked and there were Mother's ashes in it. When I saw that I felt as if I had fallen into the bottom of the sea ..."

Kiyoko says, "In front of Mother, a girl was sitting who was just about my age. Her whole body was covered with burns and wounds and she was bleeding. She seemed to be in great pain and she kept calling her mother; but all of a sudden she asked my mother, 'Please lady, is your child here?' That was because the child couldn't see any longer. Mother answered, 'Yes, she is.' Then the girl said, 'Please give this to your child,' and she held out something. It was her lunch box. It was the lunch that her mother had fixed for her and given to her that morning when she left for school. 'Don't you want to eat it yourself?' Mother asked. 'I'm going to die. Give it to your daughter.' We accepted it. For a while we went down the river and as the boat reached the sea that child said, 'Lady, I'll tell you my name and if you should meet my mother tell her that I am here, will you?' and as she said it she drew her last breath and died. I was terribly, terribly sorry for her. Mother and I wept together ..."

Both of those children, Kiyoko and the girl who lost her sight, were nine years old. Just like you back then, Mama, in Sochy.

Those children who died in the atomic apocalypse are symbolically set in the foundation of world peace. Because their fate—and naturally that of their parents—so horrified everyone, especially the Americans and the Russians, that for decades the atomic bomb has been kept on a very short leash. Those children, punished by America for Japanese war crimes, became victims of a literal holocaust—a sacrifice consumed by fire.

What is a child, anyway?

Mama, Mama, Mama. Who are you, Mama? What ties, what bonds, what belts, what straps keep us together? What guilt and punishment? I remember love from childhood, when it was still an instinct, a force of nature. You were so beautiful, so kind. Even if you got angry, you were still longed-for. When you left the house, the world collapsed. A child is like a dog who feels abandoned forever even if his guardian just goes to the store around the corner.

One morning I woke up in my room and could hear that I was alone in the apartment. The silence pushed against me from every side. From the kitchen, the bathroom, my parents' bedroom; it slipped in under the door of the apartment and brought me the terrifying news that I was ALONE. I shrank and expanded at the same time; that's very possible in our universe. I was four years old and was already able to open the window. Which I did. I knelt on the sill and saw that the sky was completely empty. Trembling with excitement, I didn't see anything else. And I wouldn't have seen anything else if I hadn't suddenly spotted you.

You were walking along the street, down the sidewalk.

You had long hair that was blowing in the wind.

You had on a light-blue dress, pleated at the waist, with a square neckline.

Your chin was tilted up as if you were looking right at me where I was kneeling, high up on the windowsill.

You were coming back.

There is life after loss, I felt after that moment. And I was filled with a wonderful light.

*

When about a month ago you had to be taken to the hospital for another operation, all the things I bought for you were light blue: robe, shirt, towel, socks, even soap and sponge. "Am I already going to heaven?" you asked in a weak voice, and I smiled at my memories ...

I would like to make sure I understand everything, discover who you are—that little girl who lost her mother and father, her entire village, her sun and her moon and all her fairy tales.

*

What is reason, what is reality for a girl who's only a few years old? A child has just a little life, on the edge, what does she know of the world? Mother and father, a few people, a yard, yesterday, and whatever is happening right now. Too short a time for her personality to have acquired concrete traits—more like a psychological cloud that, if blown on, will scatter ... or else become so deformed that it is no longer human. You know that, in Cambodia, children sell little girls to brothels? After all, what is a child? It's always easy to make another ... and that will bring in a little income, too, ten dollars a month, which in poverty-stricken Cambodia is definitely something. Cambodians have a reputation for being cruel, because of the Khmer Rouge, who killed between 1 and 2.5 million people (estimates vary), some one fifth of the population, using the cruelest methods. It is those children who witnessed the crimes back then, and who now have children of their own—children they are selling to brothels when necessary. And if the girl doesn't want to comply, the father or mother beats her into going, even if she is on her hands and knees.

And she, too, will have children.

*

In Cambodia during the reign of Pol Pot, which was not so long ago, when I was a student, people were arrested based on kinship—parents along with their children, or even grandchildren. Together they were sent into the machinery of extermination, for instance to S-21, an enormous prison, where people lay chained on the floor in large cells, each person shackled to the next. Children were torn from their mothers and killed right away behind the prison building. It was clear that everyone was slated to die, but first they needed to be interrogated. There were teams of interrogators that operated at different levels of cruelty—such as "mild," "hot," and "chewing."

The guards were teenage boys, the youngest of which were thirteen. They had been brainwashed beforehand, and so were emotionally programmed. "People who got sent there were already corpses," one former guard relates. A documentary I recently watched in the early hours of the morning shows a conversation between two survivors and some former guards. The guards are surprised at the idea they did something bad. They had their work, it was very hard, and if they shirked, they would die as well. They tell the camera what their work consisted of, playing out the encounters like a typical crime scene reconstruction. They enter the empty hall, bend over a place where a prisoner had been, say something to someone who had lain there years ago, kick him or shout at him that if he doesn't shut up he won't live to see tomorrow. They escort the prisoners in and out, undo their chains and lock them back up, open and close doors. Their bodies have memorized the motions. They are perfectly able to feel their way into a state where they feel nothing.

"What did you think," asks one of the survivors, "when you were standing over a pit in the woods, firing into the neck of your hundredth victim?"

"I didn't think. I wanted to be done with it so I could go home."

"And today, how do you live with that?"

"When I think about it, my head hurts. I go to the bar with my colleagues and get drunk. Then I quickly go to bed."

Back then they were boys who had gone through intensive training—intensive and effective. Today perhaps some among them sell their daughters to brothels. They are psychologically damaged—a young brain is malleable, and anything can be done with it. The children who came out of the camps, such as those liberated from Auschwitz, were also strange. They played prisoner and guard, scared each other by invoking the crematorium. And they were unable to cry. The young brain is malleable.

I don't know how Cambodia has settled with its past, or for whom they would do that, the break was so severe.

The basement

The basement in Sochy remained. It survived. Because it was made of stone, and carefully constructed by grandfather Władek. Only the basement and nothing else. No one had built there for forty years. Everything was overgrown with grass. Green covered what had been lost, and below that was the basement. You were very consistent about not going there. Only Anastazja went, because she kept some things in your basement in case they were needed. Her place was close by—just across the road from "your place"—except you were no longer there.

"How many meters away was that? Twenty?"

"More, because our house was back a bit, not right on the road."

*

You never wanted to see that place again, that place where you were not, that empty place where your house had been. You preferred to keep the living house in your memory, with furniture, a stove, a bench by the stove, and your mother in the kitchen and your father in the shop. You were never tempted. Do you remember the times I practically hounded you to go there? To go, at least look at the basement, look through the window—the window isn't there but you can see inside ... You didn't want to, because you're stubborn.

*

Do you know that when I was in Wrocław, living with my little children in the house I described in my book *Dziewczyna z zapałkami* (The Girl with the Matches), one day the daughter of the former German residents showed up? It was 1988. Since she was six years old in 1945, she was about fifty in 1988—an age when people start taking a hard look behind them. So she absolutely had to revisit the family home. Her real name was Barbara Jonek, not Lotta Halschke like in my novel. I named her Lotta because she had jumped from the second story, escaping from the Russians with her mother—and the leap was like a *lot*, a flight. A brave girl. She jumped and landed so well she didn't break any bones. The daughter of an ss-man ... and a Jewish mother.

And so one day in fall she climbed out of a taxi and stood at the gate of her family home in Breslau. To this day there's a plate that says *Briefe* because at one point there was a mailbox there. My mother-in-law didn't want to let her in, but the lady started asking in every language she knew—German didn't work because that was the language of the enemy, and even though my mother-in-law knew it, she refused to enter into a conversation. English was okay, but my mother-in-law kept her answers curt, using half-words. Finally, when she switched to French, my mother-in-law relented—French was close to her because she thought it was the language of the most civilized nation in the world. So, using that French filter, she managed to have a conversation with that German woman and even allowed her to walk around the house and the garden. For a whole year afterwards Barbara Jonek sent letters to Breslau, translated into Polish. Just to maintain contact. She even started to learn Polish from some pseudo-teacher, evidently a rather uneducated woman with a rough command of Polish at best, with the result that the letters were very funny:

"Lady, I want to thank you with all my Heart, that you were so wonderful and gave me the possibility the House of my Parents to see and even photograph. It was a very beautiful experience for me, I don't know how I can thank you. In this Moment when we met each other I was so nervous I didn't even introduce Myself well. My best Wish from all my Heart would be that we have Contact with each other. I would be very glad if You would write me a short Letter. Please I would be very dankful."

Such were the fates of those children from the war—both sides dogged with misfortune. Later on, those children would roam through life in search of something, checking where their crib had been, where the floorboards had creaked, and whether there wasn't a trace left on the wall where a picture had once hung. Forever unconsoled, with an unfinished past … Really, why haven't I looked her up since then, that Barbara Jonek? After all, it might be a Silesian family? And I was also born in Schlesien, as the Germans call it. Jonek is a very Silesian name. I have the letters with the sender's address, I should have done something long ago, checked to see if Barbara is still alive. If she is, I have to tell her what happened to her home later on; since it wound up being my children's home as well! Today there is a preschool there; strange, a kindergarten in a building that housed so much misfortune … I just hope that Jonek's ss father never wound up near Zamość.

*

All that's left of your home, Mama, is a basement. And really not even that, because in the end that collapsed as well. So now a couple photos are all that we have from the family that perished …

"No, there is something else. Jaś has my father's silver watch, with the chain."

"Oh, right, what's left of the entire estate is your father's watch, which by some miracle survived ... For three surviving children, six grandchildren, nine great-grandchildren, and one great-great-granddaughter. Nineteen people in all."

And of all things a watch, like a symbol of the time that was taken from them.

Landscape after annihilation

If I were narrating the film of your life ... actually that's kind of what I'm doing with this account, this memory movie, starting from the moment you were no longer in Sochy. You are in Tereszpol with your brother and sister, while I stayed here in the burned valley, walking around and looking. And here and there I see the charred chimneys sticking out over the debris of smoldering beams, the fences not fully burned, some knocked down, some still standing, and below them the bodies of those who wanted to get something, hide something, let out a cow or a horse. They're lying on their backs with outstretched arms, or on their sides with their bent knees, or with their faces to the ground. Wearing a jacket, a sweater, a dress.

Behind the shed, behind the barn whose walls have caved in and are now cooling after the fire, a woman is lying with her breast exposed, together with a child who fell from it, a child who isn't crying, who is no longer moving. Further out is a little girl with an unraveled braid; her eyes are open, her eyelids are not twitching, as though she were calmly staring at the sky, from which a strip of blue was torn off and fell right next to her. It's a ribbon for her hair she never managed to tie. Her sandals are unbuckled. Her haste no longer hurries. Further on is a man wearing a sweater that is gray except on his chest where it is red, by the entrance to the little cowshed that is no longer there. Further, a blackened figure in the outline of a bed, a burned bed in the outline of a cottage; it's almost impossible to make out the former shapes, a charcoal sketch ...

The road is pockmarked with shells and littered with wreckage. It's dry, it hasn't rained for days. No movement, no sound. Not even the burned leaves shake on the burned branch, no birds flutter past or make a peep—there are none. Some dog (not Misiek) runs across the road with his tail between his legs, but the picture sews itself up behind him and freezes. I pass the well with the charred sweep, the water not fit for taking ... Here is where you turn to go to Władek Ferenc's shop. The shop has disappeared, the house has disappeared, like everything else. Only a few brighter stones from the foundation can be seen peeking out from below in a few places. Among the timbers cooling from the fire is a broken window frame, its panes shattered, the view outside now fallen. On the ground are blackened bottles, full of orangeade and beer, a little further is a shard from one of the big jars that had once stood on the counter. The charred countertop has fallen to the ground, where it's leaning against the edge of the foundation.

Do you remember how you used to reach into the jar all the way up to your elbow to fish out a sticky candy from the very bottom, the white one with the almond flavor? There's no trace of the candies; the fire devoured them. The green paint has vanished from the shop scale, which is lying there with the pans twisted, the ebonite dishes melted into a black clod. There were large cans of kerosene, when the flames reached them they were bound to flare up enormously. And then for a few minutes your home towered over the rest of the village ... And where is Władek? He's nearby the entire time, lying on the sandy path. Through the roar of the airplanes, the crackling and rumbling of the fire. He probably didn't die right away, maybe he was unconscious, he didn't see the fire, but what if he came to a moment before he died? It was brighter than day and hotter than hell ...

Heraclitus believed that the cosmos was a living fire, which blazes up and dies down, unifying everything. A good idea for philosophy, but is it good for life?

Władek, if he did come around for a moment before dying, would have remembered for all eternity that everything he had built with such care, everything he had accumulated, had lost its shape. If he came around he might have thought about Józia and the children, about where they might be. But it's also possible that at the brink of consciousness, his final thoughts were stuck on the tin with the money, for which he had returned to the basement before instantly dropping to the ground. That would have been best for him.

Józia, after being shot in the mouth, died in a split second. I have to think she didn't suffer, so that we don't suffer. Let her lie there on the soft ground between the ears of grain, in her green scarf ... which was red at the back.

*

Count Jan Zamoyski himself—the last *ordynat* of the Zamoyski estate—went to see the village after it was razed ...

*

You are not in any condition to go back there. But I am. Because I can look at it. Because I can rummage through the burned ruins, uncovering pieces of unburned forms, gathering fragments of a fallen world, vestiges of a happier fate that was then lost in the divine lottery. I can take in with my eyes the chaos, the ruins, the ashes, and with my ears I can penetrate the silence that follows the end of the world, I can feel the bitterness that nothing can extinguish, and which I'd gladly stuff down the good Lord's throat, if He were here.

Clearly it's me that can do this, and not you. I can manage. I'm a brave boy, Mama. You're a little girl who's been afraid her whole life and who has always spread her fear. So what that you wrote all those poems about your mother, your father, your home, and your village that was utterly destroyed? Those human, childish sorrows ... You didn't fight, you didn't join some protest, you didn't hurl curses, you didn't say, "I prefer the devil because God didn't pass the test," you didn't want revenge, you didn't go to the Germans to have them pay for your house, the store, for your mother and your father. Didn't make them pay you for the weeks you had no voice, the years of constant crying, the hunger day after day, for being worked to exhaustion, for a childhood spent in orphanages, for nightmares, for your mother's green scarf, which is all you remember of her. Mama, these days people sue each other for trivial things. Because they smoked a cigarette in good faith, or ate a pill that made an eyelash fall out ... And, for the loss of one's fate? Think about how much you could get for that. That would be a trial for the whole world to see at the European court in Strasbourg. Damn it.

*

Renia, Jaś, Kropka, Stasia, Bronka, Danusia, Stasio— many with that name—two Władeks, Franko, one Henio and another very little Henio as well, Rysio, Janka, Czesia, Julka, and Julek who was called Romek, Tadek, Hela, Gienia, Marysia, Stefka ... How many of those orphaned children stayed in Sochy? I'd have to count them. Nearly all their fathers were shot, but a few of the mothers survived. Many children died, the ones who were killed in their parents' arms may have been a little less scared. Stefka lost her father, her mother was wounded and then caught typhus after the fire but still she managed to survive; she was the one who cried when she awakened her children to the worst day of their life. And Stefka was the only one from Sochy who wound up in Majdanek …

For many years the orphaned children lived in basements, in huts, in dugouts, hastily rigged shacks, "modernized" pigpens, before they grew up and started building homes similar to the ones they had had. For years they lived in extreme poverty. It was a good thing the Zamoyskis gave some assistance right after the fire. Count Zamoyski arrived to organize aid for the group of people left among the charred remains, dazed with horror. He designated a spot in the cemetery, and then Róża Zamoyska sent clothing and food. It was as much as they could do in that sea of misfortune—the war was still going on, the terror was getting worse, and the hunger was increasing, because the Germans were ratcheting up the requisitions.

Those were wonderful people, the Zamoyskis. What they did for "their" villages, for the children in the camp at Zwierzyniec, was so miraculous that Hollywood ought to make a movie about them. And they'd come out well on film because, apart from being good and brave, they were also good-looking. Their house in Zwierzyniec, where they lived during the war, was very pretty, a kind of villa. I went to see it. Today it serves as an orphanage.

It would be the way a documentary ought to be: the picturesque Roztocze landscape, the home with the classical architecture, the storms of war, and an aristocratic couple recently married and very much in love. He, the last *ordynat*; she, the daughter of a princess. And if it were all too perfect, something could be found, some blemish, to make them a little more human ... They risked the concentration camp (where Róża's father died, by the way) but they saved who they could, devotedly and also intelligently, with a plan. Count Zamoyski rescued hundreds of children who were dying of hunger and disease in the camp. He managed to negotiate with Odilo Globocnik, the loutish head of the Lublin SS. And then directly with Hauptsturmführer Hahn, the camp commandant. A wondrously smart approach! He prepared a speech which was a veritable diplomatic slalom ("I know that the Great German Reich does not wage war against children and is able to show generosity to those creatures who are not guilty but who must bear suffering on account of their elders ...") And with that he even managed to convince Globocnik. For Hahn he furnished some brandy, smoked meat, wine, coffee. To each according to his needs ...

He and Róża set up four children's hospitals. Every Polish town ought to have a street named after them, no question about it. Why aren't there any? And why isn't there yet a film about them, considering that these are heroes of mythic proportions? The storyline is clearly there. I don't understand ... Was this annihilation too little? Their heroism not enough? And the fact that they stayed in communist Poland, where they had to struggle with the rough and sour realities instead of escaping to the West to join their high-born relatives.

*

"You know I went to that Róża's house ..."
"Really, Mama? When were you there?"
"Before the fire, my mother took me when she went

there. She spoke with Pani Zamoyska a couple times about something. One time, I remember, we took a bucket of strawberries. Or maybe they were cherries ... Mama went inside while I played outside on the grass with a little boy. I think it was their son."

"That's impossible, Mama. Their son wasn't born until after the war. Most likely that was the son of the cook or a servant girl ..."

"Anyway, some boy was there, more or less my age, and at some point Pani Róża called him, and she came out to us on the porch."

*

That someone wasn't their son, because the Zamoyskis married in 1938, and their son was born two years after the war, in Sopot. When he was still in his diapers, the socialist fatherland put his father behind bars for eight years—for his actions during the war with the Home Army resistance. That's a real historical chortle, isn't it? From time to time history changes into a genuine psychopath who enjoys being amused by tragic absurdities ... But perhaps the Swiss could make the film about them, if the Poles don't want to, because after he got out of prison Jan Zamoyski worked for the Swiss airline ... *The Last Ordynat*—that has a nice ring. There's a book of conversations with him with that same title. Thank God someone managed at least that before he died. What a country ...

Ich erzähle

Staszka, who still lives in Sochy, and whose father was the village leader, put it like this to me: "Those of us who remember tell about it, and when we die, our children won't tell about it, because they didn't want to listen. They said: that's impossible. They said: What planet were you living on? Why on earth did you wait for them to come and kill you? Because how can you just lie down on the ground for them to shoot you?"

Exactly. Who can understand death?

Those who haven't started dying, and those who never came close to death's door, view death as simply a word. A word whose letters are mixed with fear, but nonetheless only a word. Imagination doesn't help and neither does a convincing context; empathy cannot reflect that particular experience, its terrible gravitas, its absolute otherness from all other experiences that occur at some safe distance from its borders, from the edge of existence.

Because, for the children of Sochy, their tragedy didn't fit the model of deportation, they didn't receive the same official designation as the "Children of Zamojszczyzna" who were deported to the Reich for slave labor, sent to concentration camps, or selected for "Germanization." Consequently, the survivors of Sochy never received any compensation. Letters and petitions sent to the authorities were returned with the notice that there was no basis. There are different types of crimes, and massacre doesn't fall into the category of deportation trauma ...

The people from Sochy never cried out their hatred,

they didn't shed their fear, and they didn't receive any satisfaction from justice being done, which in their case never happened. No one helped them either psychologically or materially. The children who were missing both parents wound up in orphanages, and that was what happened to you, while those who were lucky enough to have a mother spent the rest of their childhood in Sochy, forgotten by history as it is officially recorded. Once upon a time a massacre took place there, and that was that. A few hours for a whole life. But that massacre didn't qualify for anything. Something apparently didn't go right. Sure, the Germans shot the villagers, they set houses on fire and bombed whatever was still standing, but it was just a small village: eighty-eight homes, a couple hundred people. Apparently the name shows up in a few books along with the observation that it was the most horrible massacre in the Zamość region, comparable to Oradour or Lidice, but at most it's merely a footnote.

*

Why did they forgive? Why in our name? What right did they have? Uncle Jaś asked me. The people from Sochy ask the same thing—those children now in old people's bodies, who lived to see the famous day of reconciliation in Krzyżowa on November 12, 1989, when Prime Minister Mazowiecki and Chancellor Kohl exchanged the sign of peace. Earlier, in 1965, when the Polish bishops sent a letter to the German bishops with the famous sentence: "We forgive and ask for forgiveness," the former children of Sochy were in their prime, and their bitterness was alive and strong. Simple people who couldn't understand why no one had asked their opinion, why there hadn't been a referendum ... But then again, the victims' point of view is seldom a good place of departure in politics. So they are not consulted, and gestures are made on the international stage which promise some greater benefit. Meanwhile all we are left with is a wholesale account, a general eulogy to the ruins of hundreds of towns and villages, to the millions of victims.

*

On November 17, 2010, Bernd Posselt, speaker of the Sudeten German Homeland Association and former member of the European Parliament, bowed his head in memory of those murdered in Lidice and asked for forgiveness "for that part of the guilt that we bear." Divvying the guilt like that is a pretty clever idea.

Because how much can be bestowed on the Germans? Especially when we consider the fact that the Waffen-ss and the Wehrmacht were full of non-Germans, various "sympathizers" from foreign tribes who did not meet the required standards of height, whose morphology did not fit the ideology ... particularly towards the end of the war. As a matter of fact, the Germans took nearly every European nation into their army: Hungarians, Romanians, French, Dutch, Swedes, Norwegians, Lithuanians, Latvians, Muslim Bosnians, and Slavs in general ... Even some Jews fought shoulder to shoulder with groups aligned with Hitler against the allies—for instance in the Finnish army, where Jews were treated as people and fairly drafted into the ranks of an army that fought alongside the fascists.

Of course, if the guilt is shared, then it follows that the punishment, too, is apportioned ... and that can lead to rather perfidious twists of history. Because weren't the Poles punished for the war in which they were among the victors, and earlier the victims? After the Allies sold us to the Soviets at Yalta, in return for our brave fighting on many fronts ...

Meanwhile West Germany was rewarded, because the division of Germany in 1949 had the result that one part of Germany won while another part lost. Those who wound up in West Germany were the real victors—they won the war, since they soon received solid American support, which allowed them to lick their wounds and return to prosperity and well-being at breakneck speed. They could afford the luxury of introspection, and for a while they examined their collective guilt with discussions in the press, etc. The losing East Germans, on the other hand, wound up attached to the Slavs. Imagine the loss of dignity, the degradation—being forced into the same community as the recently designated subhumans, having to submit to the reviled Bolshevism—that was their punishment for supporting Hitler. So half of the Germans (really a third), the East Germans, didn't have any problem with the guilt, but rather with the punishment. The poor citizens rode in their cardboard Trabants on vacation to Poland, because it was cheaper here. And whether we like it or not, they, like us, are among the losers of the war, whatever they write in the textbooks.

Uncle Jaś told me that the German language has always caused him to panic. Sometimes he's felt the panic before he's even realized what's going on. For instance on the beach—he'll be looking out at the sea, his back to the sun, and all of a sudden he senses that something isn't right, that something is pressing against him, piling on top of him in the clear air. An irrational fear takes hold. And an overpowering urge to escape. Only when he starts to calm down and take a few deep breaths does he discern some fragments of sentences coming from a nearby blanket. It turns out some Germans are sitting there, talking in their language. Jaś has German so deeply embedded in his brain that he registers it before he realizes it ... Although he doesn't speak German at all, in some sense he knows it better than his native tongue.

Mazowiecki forgave Kohl, but Jaś hasn't forgiven the Germans, he is physically incapable, his Slavic organism is afraid of those German organisms that emit Germanic sounds. That is the "psychopolitical" state of former victims, independent of their will.

*

I also inherited that dislike for the German language, which is personally unfair of me as well as historically unjust, because it is a beautiful language of writers and philosophers I admire. It's also the language of Schubert's Lieder, which entranced me once I was grown up. My father speaks German very well, he survived the war in Bydgoszcz, was a pupil in the Grundschule in Bromberg, and the German words were so deeply etched into his memory that they're there to this day. But I was unable to hold on to them ... And I tried so many times. Always new teachers, new courses or private lessons. German was offered in my high school, my accent and pronunciation were very good, but there wasn't anything to pronounce, because whatever I learned I immediately forgot. It was because of German that I almost had to repeat my third year of high school. My father teased me that after all those years of study the only sentence I retained was: *ich habe etwas Zeit, ich kann dir es erzählen* (I have a little time, I can tell you about it.)

And that's exactly what I'm doing, telling and telling, to you and to me. So that it will be remembered.

The end

You've forgotten many things, Mama, and there were many things you didn't ever know. You didn't even know everything about Sochy, you were so afraid to go back there in your thoughts. Not to mention the rest of the war.

"No one ever talked about what happened, after the war, with you children?"

"No, it was a taboo subject."

"To the point where I don't know if I should talk about it with you now ... Maybe I'm unnecessarily turning over stones that have already grown into the ground. You know that in Międzyrzec, where you wound up after Zamość and before Biała Podlaska ... were you in three orphanages altogether?"

"In three."

"So, in Międzyrzec in 1942 they killed very many Jewish children, did you all know about that?"

"No, none of the grown-ups ever went back to those topics, children were supposed to be happy at last. And that was my best orphanage."

Well, I'll tell you something about Fela and Karol Szponar (house 48), they died from a single bullet: she covered him with her own body when the German aimed, she couldn't imagine living without him. Later, when she was dying in her own mother's arms, she asked her mother to raise their one-and-a-half-year-old son. "Bring him up," she said, and then she confessed her sins to her mother. "I'll tell you everything," she whispered, because she was losing her strength, "and you go to church and confess on my behalf for the absolution." That little boy, Rysio, sobbed and sobbed for months on end. He bawled so horribly that no one could stand it. People ran away from him and covered their ears. Maybe he was hungry, since there wasn't anything to eat ... Maybe he was hungry for his mother. And maybe that child had gone crazy from what he saw. Finally the other son-in-law who had survived couldn't stand it and one day said, "I'm going to work, and when I come back that Rysio better be gone." And then that grandmother—what was the poor woman to do—went to the priest in Tereszpol so he could help find some new place, because otherwise something bad was going to happen. And the priest helped.

*

The children from Sochy had various fates. Some were ultimately placed in shelters or in orphanages after the war, which, although poor, did offer some warmth and some surrogate community—although not like the ones today. At night the children cried into their pillows, dreaming for a miracle to happen so their mothers would come back. Or at least that some relative, someone they knew from the village, would come and visit ... Every little unpleasantness sparked the same thought: "If my mother were here she wouldn't have allowed that ..." That's what Kropka told me. She's longed for her mother her whole life, even though all she remembers of her is the green scarf.

The sadness that is inherent in communities of children is something that cannot be removed, despite the fact that children are capable of adapting to almost every situation, due to their survival instinct. The sore spots get covered with a psychological scab and one just has to be careful that it doesn't get scraped away. I remember you once told me that when you were in the orphanage in Zamość a relative came to visit from Ruszów, some distant aunt, no one you knew well, but you were still in class when she showed up. She didn't wait, she just left a box of pastries and left. You didn't want them, you cried at the box as if something terrible had happened.

*

Some of the Sochy children grew up with distant relatives, if the latter could afford it, or if they needed extra hands for work. Some wound up with complete strangers, like Aunt Agnieszka's sons, your father's sister who was also killed. Bronka Szawara put it this way: "They loaded those children onto the train and the railroad workers divvied them up, whoever wanted one took one. The oldest, Władek, he stayed in Szozdy; Romek went to Hedwiżyn; and Janek and Heniek, who were very small, got taken to Biłgoraj." Because some relative of their father's lived there. Their father was an interesting man, too, seldom at home, always traveling around going from village to village with magic tricks, pulling rabbits out of hats, money out of a sleeve. And this one time he just happened to be coming back to Sochy and got caught in the pacification a stroke of bad luck. He died and never learned that one of his sons who survived went on to become the director of a large automobile factory and then moved to America. It's a shame that those murdered parents never saw how resourceful their children turned out to be.

*

Do you know, Mama, how Bronka managed? She stayed in the burned-out village, she was strong, almost sixteen years old. First she and her sister stayed in Rudka, with her aunt Hałasicha, but it was very cramped and there was no food, their uncle kept going on about them having nothing to eat and no place to sit. Because only the kitchen was finished. And her aunt barely managed to fix them something to eat. She would take a handful of grain and grind it up into a kind of paste and boil it. "I couldn't bear the sight of it," says Bronka, "and at Christmas I decided to do something. I went to another aunt in Bukownica; the Germans had taken all her people apart from her son Antek, and he was hiding in the forest. So I went to her place and cried because I didn't know exactly what to do and I had to do something. This Antek showed up from the forest and asked, why are you sitting there in the dark? Well, because there was nothing to light. Don't cry, child, says Antek, I'll talk with Franek Szydełko. Mama, I'm talking about that little pen where the hens are now, Franek and I will take it apart and bring it to Sochy then build it up and I'll stay there. Because I don't know what else to do. And that's what happened. When March came, Marysia and I moved from Rudka to Sochy and we stayed in that pen. It was tiny, a little kitchen with a tiny larder, but it was our own. Then others moved in with us, an aunt with a child, little Heniek, then Kryśka and Janka, because they didn't have a roof either, all out in some hut. Whoever could fit in would come inside to get warmed up. Because we had a stove right away, with a little area set off for the children, for Marysia and little Heniek, they had a tiny place on the stove for sitting."

Staszka had it worse, because they lived in a "dugout"— Aunt Anastazja, the pretty one, and her children and your grandfather. The dugout was a kind of basement; they made some tiered bunks and put down some straw and that was that. The stove was up above them; they put down some boards so Grandfather could sleep there and stretch his legs—he was already old, he wouldn't have managed in the basement. He lived another two years. Bronka didn't have a bed or bedding either, everything was burned. Janek Żołdak made a floor for them, "smoothed out the splinters," and they slept on the floor under a single blanket someone had given them. Up to the moment that old Magda showed up and said, "So what that you have a floor and a table made out of a few boards—you don't have a bed and what are you doing with just one blanket? But it doesn't matter, let's get some straw and I'll fix you up with something that will be so warm you'll all be sweating."

"And that's what happened," said Bronka. "That old Magda brought some fabric from the Żołdaks and then Rybak's wife gave another piece—old gray linen, coarsely woven. And Magda came and sewed it up. Then she sent us onto the wet meadow for those cattails that grow there in the reeds. And we picked them and brought them in—we had to make two trips because they were heavy. Then she spent the evening pulling those cattails completely apart like down and stuffing them into those sheets. We ran some stitches with a linen thread across so that fluff wouldn't bunch up in the middle. And we had a down blanket made of cattails. And it was so warm, so warm that the children weren't cold and neither were we. But when we got up in the morning our hair was all matted. Because when that fluff crumbled up and got into those little hairs, what with the fabric so coarse, well, it all seeped out ... And that little Henio, when he'd grown a little, used to tell everyone he was born in a pile of lint."

I'm telling you, Mama, you ought to hear those stories! She and Staszka sat there in the small room at the old table, with the sun going down in the window, so that everything turned red, and then the light faded and faded and they kept remembering things and laughing and crying, laughing and crying—they completely forgot about me, and it was getting darker and darker. It wasn't just sunset but some kind of primal evening; there was something eternal in it, something of the old village get-togethers when people would just be together, outside of time, living life as it was, is, and will be, alongside death, which for all eternity is in a race with that same life.

Those two women, old and young at the same time, and in some moments still children, but wise with the knowledge that matures in a person on its own, growing from year to year like the rings of a tree ...

Until finally all I could see were shadows and all I could hear was a whisper, just as if I had become tiny and was falling asleep in a cradle, more and more groggy, but sated and soothed. At last returned and reconciled.

*

Forget. It's better now that you should forget. You're doing well to lose your memory, the names are disappearing one by one. The pictures on your internal screen are fading, they're all burned out. The cinema of your brain is getting quieter and quieter ... You're no longer tossing and turning, going up and down, you're not having fits of helpless melancholy alternating with inconceivable fury. You are increasingly calm, steady, level. You are leaving, Mama. What's left is peace.

And me. I've taken your story, Mama, your apocalypse. You fed it to me when I was little, a tiny pinch at a time, so as not to poison me completely. But it added up. I have it in my blood. For decades it has darkened my image of the world. Today it may be more in me than in you. My whole life I've held back from living because I was waiting for war. I don't want to go on like that anymore …

What am I supposed to do with our story now? My children don't want it.

I'll put it into airtight sentences, closed paragraphs. So that no smoke or flame or tears will appear. And so you won't have to take it into the next world. And after everything I will write the words:

THE END.

PHILIP BOEHM is an American playwright, theater director, and literary translator whose career has zigzagged across languages, borders, and cultural divides. He studied at the State Academy of Theater in Warsaw, Poland, and has directed extensively on both sides of the Atlantic. He has translated more than thirty novels and plays, mostly by German and Polish writers including Herta Müller, Franz Kafka, and Hanna Krall. For this work he has received numerous awards, including fellowships from the NEA and the John Simon Guggenheim Memorial Foundation.